THE ZETA TEAM

D.J. GOODMAN

SEVERED PRESS
HOBART TASMANIA

THE ZETA TEAM

Copyright © 2017 D.J. Goodman
Copyright © 2017 by Severed Press

WWW.SEVEREDPRESS.COM

All rights reserved. No part of this book may be
reproduced or transmitted in any form or by any
electronic or mechanical means, including
photocopying, recording or by any information and
retrieval system, without the written permission of
the publisher and author, except where permitted by law.
This novel is a work of fiction. Names,
characters, places and incidents are the product of
the author's imagination, or are used fictitiously.
Any resemblance to actual events, locales or persons,
living or dead, is purely coincidental.

ISBN: 978-1-925597-73-8

All rights reserved.

1

Marco Cruz knew exactly what was about to happen. He stood at attention, waiting for it with his eyes straight ahead, hands at his sides, feet together, uniform immaculately clean. On the inside he wanted to scream, maybe even break down and cry. But he had known for some time that this was going to happen, so he had prepared himself. He would face his discharge with grace and dignity. He would continue to act as the dutiful soldier, all the way up until the point where he wasn't one anymore.

He'd been standing like this for nearly a minute, now. Colonel Horitz sat at his desk, just as still as Marco, his trademark scowl plastered on his leathery face. Marco resisted the urge to look around the colonel's office, although he had immediately seen more than enough details that he got a feel for the way the man lived outside of his home life. Horitz was fastidious. There was not a spot of dust anywhere, despite the rumors that cleaning people weren't allowed in his office. There were a few plaques on the walls, as well as a degree in business management, for some reason. There were exactly two pictures hanging up, one on each wall to Marco's sides. The only other decorative piece in the entire room was a mounted shark's tooth of unusual size. Marco's brain worked, trying to put all these details together to get a better idea of Horitz as a colonel rather than when he was a civilian, but he wasn't able to concentrate on that today. For once, his brain was actually staying where it should, rather than wandering off on him. Too bad it hadn't been able to play nice with him before this. Then, maybe, he wouldn't be about to be kicked out of the Interplanetary Army.

"At ease, soldier," Horitz finally said. Marco switched to at-rest posture, yet continued to keep his eyes straight ahead.

"Do you know why you're here, Private Cruz?"

Marco swallowed before answering. "Sir, yes sir."

Horitz sighed. "Son, let's cut the crap. We both know as of a few minutes from now, you're not going to need to call me 'sir' anymore. You won't even need to call me Colonel. You might as well just go back to calling me Jake."

Marco finally let his eyes meet Horitz's. "Sir, if it's all the same to you, I'm still a soldier until you sign the discharge paperwork. I may be a screw up, but up until then I still have a duty to uphold."

Horitz sighed again. "Damn it. You're really not going to make this easy, are you?" His tone wasn't that of an angry officer scolding a subordinate. It was more like a father getting ready to ground a favorite child. "Marco, just what the hell happened? How did we get to this point?"

"It's all in the paperwork in front of you, sir."

"Yes, I know. I've read it all several times. What I want is to hear you say it. I want to know why you personally believe you're about to washout of the military."

Marco opened his mouth, but nothing came out. He really wished he could give the colonel a detailed, point-by-point analysis of how his dream of serving his planet and his system had gone terribly, horribly wrong, but if he had been able to do that, maybe he would have been able to prevent it. Finally he said, "I did the absolute best that I was capable of, sir. That's all I can say in my defense."

Horitz stood up and rubbed his temple as though trying to massage away a headache. "You had no trouble in basic, Marco. None. You weren't exactly exemplary, of course. No one ever expected great things of you. Good things, though, maybe that you could do. We all knew you would never be more than a grunt, but you at least looked like you could be a capable one."

Marco couldn't answer. He'd often thought that others might think of him this way. This was the first time he'd heard it said out loud. He wasn't sure what was worse: that the brass had decided early on that he would never be more than just adequate, or the fact that he had somehow failed at even that.

Horitz touched the small holo-file sheet on his desk, which lit the air up in front of them both with a series of reports in bright blue light. "Your first deployment. You were at Zedcron. Pretty simple, Marco. Little more than guard duty. Do you want to explain what happened there?"

"Sir, it's in the report."

"Say it. Say it out loud."

Marco gulped. "I was sure the creatures were looking at me funny, sir."

Horitz shook his head. "Zedcron is mostly a farming world. They rely on livestock. It was previously the home of over eight thousand chickens. Eight. Thousand. Do you know how many are living on the planet now?"

"Uh, eight, sir."

"Actually, it's seven now, but that last one has nothing to do with you. That was some local fox-like creature. The other seven-thousand, nine-hundred and ninety-two, though, were your fault. How the hell?"

"Er, one of the local scientists tried to explain it to me, sir, but I could barely understand him, the way he was laughing so hard."

"And that was just your first screw-up, Marco. Do you want me to go over all the other ones?"

"That's your prerogative, sir, but I hope you understand if I say I'd rather you didn't."

"I don't have to give details. All I need to do is give planet names. Waxton, Murphy, Loki…"

"With all due respect, sir, Loki wasn't my fault."

"No, I suppose not. But we both know you somehow managed to make everything worse there. And then of course there was Hicks."

Marco's stoic face couldn't prevent his cringe. Everyone had to mention what happened on Planet Hicks.

"I don't even know where to begin with Hicks," Horitz said. "Let's just say that, before you, it was generally believed that super-iron couldn't melt, period. Now, of course, we know better. Maybe the Interplanetary Army should be thanking you. At least now we know super-iron's weakness just in case any of our enemies ever steal the formula from us. In fact, that's the only thing that's saving you today."

Marco's breath caught in his throat. "Saving me, sir?"

Horitz turned off the holo-file and walked around to sit on the front of his desk. It was such a casual move, the kind of thing no one in the Interplanetary Army had ever seen from the man. At least, not while Horitz was on duty. Marco himself had seen it plenty of times back when Horitz would visit Marco's house when he was a teenager. Back then, to Marco, he really had just been Jake, the one man that finally did right by his long-suffering mother.

"Okay," Horitz said. "Maybe not the only thing. I did make a promise to your mother before she died that I would look after you. But I have to be honest, son. You sure have made that really hard for me to do."

Marco nodded. He didn't think he needed to explain to Horitz why he had wanted to be here. Horitz had seen the look in Marco's eyes often enough. It was the look of someone who had always desperately wanted a father figure, and when that father figure had finally come along, Marco had wanted to be like him in every way. With his mother dead and his father vanished into the depths of space a long time ago, Jacob Horitz was the closest thing Marco had left to family.

"Tell me something, Marco," Horitz said. All signs of the commanding officer fell away from Horitz's face. This was no longer a discussion between a colonel and a private. This was a heart to heart between a man and the person that might as well have been his son. "I know you joined up because you wanted to make me proud. And I certainly was that you wanted to serve. But when it became blindingly obvious that you didn't belong here, why did you stay?"

"Sir, I…"

"Knock it off, Marco."

Marco took a deep breath and tried again. "Jake, this is all I wanted to become. I don't even know what else there is out there that I could do. This is the only life I know, and the only one I ever wanted to know."

Horitz nodded as he slipped off his desk and then walked back around to the other side. "I can see that. But son, there's a problem. There's an old saying. Oftentimes people say it was Einstein that said it, but it wasn't. The saying goes that everyone is a genius, but if you do nothing but judge a fish by its ability to climb a tree, it will spend its entire life thinking it's an idiot. You familiar with that one?"

"I think I've heard it once or twice."

"Marco, you're a fish. You're a fish that saw a bird flying through the sky and thought that was what it meant to be successful and free. You need to stop trying to fly, and start learning to swim before it's too late."

"I'm afraid I don't follow you."

"I'll give you an example. Have you ever been in this room before today? The honest truth, now."

"No, sir."

"Good, because if you had I would need to fire someone. You walked into this room, you came right up to my desk, and you looked directly at me. Is that correct?"

"Yes, sir."

"And I've been watching you ever since. Your eyes have not left me once."

"I'm still afraid I don't understand your point."

The seriousness returned to Horitz's face as he gazed directly into Marco's eyes. "Now keep looking at me. Don't move your eyes at all. Without looking anywhere but at me, tell me what's on the picture on the wall to your right."

This was obviously some kind of test. Marco didn't understand it in the slightest, but he followed Horitz's orders exactly. "It's a picture of you shaking hands with Prime World Director Mumbe. She's with her wife. It looks like it was taken at the 2253 Ansel Peace Conference."

"Keep looking at me. What color dress is Director Mumbe wearing?"

"Blue and orange. The colors of her home world."

"And her wife. What's her wife wearing?"

"A red sarong. But she's..." Marco stopped, realizing what he had just been about to say, and understanding at the same time the point Horitz had been trying to make.

Horitz smirked. "Finish it, son. I'm sure you're about to say something quite interesting."

"Uh, yes sir. Director Mumbe's wife was cheating on her at the time. Or at least they were semi-separated. Something like that."

Horitz didn't look surprised. "And just why do you think that?"

"Her wife's wedding ring. It's gone from her finger, but there's clearly a worn spot on her finger where she was wearing it recently."

"You just stumbled upon a long-held state secret, Marco. It was actually Director Mumbe who was cheating. Her wife found out right before the peace conference. They pretended everything was fine, but she refused to wear her wedding ring as a sign of protest. Now here's the real question, Marco. You saw all that. But how long have you looked at that picture?"

"Sir, I saw it for maybe half a second on my way in."

"And yet you got all those details. Do you finally understand what I'm saying, son? You are special. You have a gift. And the Interplanetary Army is the wrong place for that gift. I wasn't joking when I said earlier that the higher brass want to give you one more chance. But what I'm saying right now is that I don't think you should take it. You'll have this discharge on your record, but I can get you into other places. Places where your peculiar eye for details won't be wasted. Now what would you say to that?"

Marco knew the offer was good. But he also knew his heart. "I would say I don't want to get into other places. I would say I want to take that last chance and prove to you that I can be a soldier."

Horitz gave yet another long-suffering sigh. "And of course I knew you were going to say that. I honest to God hoped you wouldn't, but I knew anyway."

The colonel opened a drawer in his desk to take out another holo-file sheet. He set it on top of the first and tapped it. Instead of incident reports, this one bloomed with a swirling image of a small planetoid. "Private Marco Cruz, a spot has opened up in a very special task force known as the Zeta Team." He said the words as if they were appearing on a holo-prompter that only he could see. "I have been authorized to offer you this spot as your one last chance to avoid being forcibly discharged from the Interplanetary Army." The planet vanished and was replaced with a plain, flat blue box hanging in the air. "If you accept, place your hand in the box where your handprint and DNA scan will act as your signature. If not, tell me now, and we can continue with your discharge paperwork."

Marco didn't even stop to think. He placed his left hand in the box, which glowed and burned the image of his complete handprint in the air.

Horitz shook his head as he turned off the holo-file. "I really hate when they make me say that garbage."

"Sir," Marco said. Despite his best discipline, he couldn't restrain a smile from growing on his face. "I swear that I won't let you down on this."

"No," Horitz said tiredly. "I'm sure you won't."

2

Marco woke from hyper-stasis with a renewed vigor he hadn't felt in a long time. If his pod had woken him up, then that meant that the troop shuttle *Milwaukee* was almost at their destination. He was about to be delivered to his new post. It was most certainly his most important post, too, because if he didn't treat it as such, it would end up being his *last* post.

For every other assignment, Private Cruz had been told well in advance where he was going and what would be expected of him when he got there. For the first time, though, no one had said anything to him as he'd left Captain Horitz's office to immediately be prepped for the journey. As he left his pod and hurriedly got dressed in his combat uniform, Marco let his mind race at all the possibilities of why he might have been kept in the dark. Obviously, whatever this planet was that he was going to and whatever the Zeta Team was, they were a secret. It was actually an honor. Marco didn't know how Horitz had managed to get him what was obviously going to be a very important job as his last shot, but he was grateful. There would be no screw-ups this time. He wouldn't let his mind play tricks on him like it had every other time, telling him that all the tiny extra details he saw without actually seeing them were signs of danger. He would get it all right, and he would show command that his proper place in the universe was with the Interplanetary Army.

A deep, dark part of his mind told him that he was being foolish, that certain tiny details in everything he had seen so far let him know that this was not the assignment he was assuming it to be, but Marco did his best to ignore that part of him. It had gotten him in trouble before, and he wouldn't let it get him in trouble now.

Once he was fully dressed and equipped, ready enough that he could go into combat right out of the door, Marco made his way to the cockpit. The pilot was the only other person aboard the ship. His pod had been right in the cockpit, and he didn't even bother to get out of his tank-top and boxer shorts as he took a seat at the controls. Usually these things had a co-pilot as well, but in the co-pilot's place was a holographic, semi-autonomous AI. In reality, the AI was all the ship actually needed. The pilot was just there so there would be a human to react to any mistakes the AI might make on take-off or landing. The AI, of course, never made mistakes, so the pilots on these transports were little more than glorified babysitters for robots made out of blue light.

The AI ignored Marco completely while the pilot gave Marco a lazy wave, then sleepily scratched his chest. The pilot chuckled when he saw the way Marco was dressed.

"Ah," he said. "One of those. Haven't seen one like you in a while. This ought to make things interesting down there for a week."

"What do you mean?" Marco asked.

"Don't worry about it," the pilot said. "You'll see soon enough."

"So you do this run often?"

"Heh. I wouldn't say often. There aren't exactly a lot of people who make it as far as Zeta Team. I only have to do this run once every two years or so."

That figure caught Marco's attention. "So you mean I will probably be here for at least two years?" He tried not to sound too happy about that. It was unbecoming for a soldier to feel like job security was important to them.

"I didn't say that," the pilot said. "I said I only come back every two years or so. There's one other pilot that does troop transport for here, if it's needed." The pilot chuckled as though there were something very funny about this. "And there's also the supply ship that runs once every five or six months. Once in a while there will be an additional ship for whatever or whoever the scientists need, but that isn't needed as much as it used to be."

"Scientists?" Marco asked. "Is this some kind of research facility?"

The pilot laughed so hard he started coughing. When he finally caught his breath, Marco asked, "Did I say something funny?"

"Probably not to you, kid. But to me, sure. You must be one of those ones that doesn't know what you're about to get in to, right?"

"I suppose not."

"Hey, vIdI!" the pilot called to the AI. "I'm assuming someone left some kind of 'training' holo for the kid to watch?"

Marco was never very good at reading personal signals from people, but even he could detect the sarcasm in the pilot's voice when he said "training." That nagging feeling grew in him, and this time he wasn't able to push it away.

"Yes, of course," vIdI the AI said. "Colonel Jacob Horitz transmitted this message to the ship shortly after you both went into hyper-stasis."

The viewscreen in front of them had previously shown a rapidly approaching planetoid. It was replaced by a three-dimensional shot of Horitz. "Private Marco Cruz, I want to apologize to you. Usually Major Stonewerth is the one to give the orientation for Zeta Team, but I thought I owed it to you to do this as personally as possible. If I could be there in person to give you this information, then I would, but protocol typically states that members of Zeta Team are to keep all this information top secret. And while I'm sure the mention of a top secret assignment might appeal to you, you should realize that this is probably not at all the redeeming assignment you thought it was."

Marco found himself automatically going into attention, despite the fact that Horitz wasn't actually there, and the pilot probably couldn't care less. The standard, stoic pose was more to help Marco from showing his crushing disappointment.

"You have been assigned to protection detail on Planetoid 54174340," Horitz's recording said.

"Just a number?" Marco asked. Then, when he remembered that the holo-recording couldn't answer, he directed the question at the pilot. "Doesn't it have an actual name?"

"Well, it has a nickname," the pilot said with a smirk, "but nothing command would ever publicly approve of."

"Near the end of the third wave of colonial expansion," holo-Horitz said, "a standard recon probe discovered the planetoid, recorded a few basics about it, and then continued on. When the data was finally analyzed, however, scientists with the Prime World Union discovered a few shocking peculiarities. 54174340 orbits a Class D star and is smaller than even Luna, so there is no reason it should be capable of supporting life. And yet it has a near Earth-standard gravity and an atmosphere that, while not completely ideal, is still enough to support humanoid life. It also periodically emits bizarre static charges into space. In short, it's an impossible little world, and science teams were immediately dispatched to study it, with a heavy support team of the Interplanetary Army's best troops."

Marco almost let himself feel pride that he was about to be part of such a prestigious operation, yet he had figured out by now that the other shoe still had to drop. This place might be amazing, but there was a reason Horitz seemed to consider it a punishment assignment.

"A small number of alien ruins were discovered," Horitz said. "These were the source of the electrical discharges. I'm sure you can appreciate why this caused excitement."

Damned straight, Marco could understand. Aliens. Real, honest to God aliens. Scientists still occasionally released small amounts of information that they said proved that, at least at one point in time, a number of colonial worlds had once been the home of intelligent species other than humans. But all that was mostly academic, and the average person didn't understand the complex reasoning scientists gave for their beliefs. But actual ruins, those were a different thing altogether.

"Planetoid 54174340 was immediately declared a state secret until it could be properly studied, and the Interplanetary Army set up a base. Now, given how peculiar you are with details, you've already figured out the problem here."

Well, that wasn't the way Marco's gift worked. It was like his mind stored every detail, but he didn't recall them and instantly analyze them until he made the effort. Now that Horitz did say there was an issue, Marco's brain immediately went over what the colonel had said, cross-referenced it with what he knew of history, and he saw what was wrong. They were currently in what was being called the Fifth Wave of Colonial Expansion. The Third Wave had been nearly a century ago, in Earth-standard years. Which meant...

"The scientists found nothing," Horitz said. "I'm sure I don't need to give you details, as you'll learn all of them soon enough, but they were stumped. The ruins on 54174340 are still unique, and nothing else similar has ever been found. Because of their nature, they are still considered secret. But because they resist categorization, no progress has been made, and the Interplanetary Army has reduced its presence on the planetoid over the years. What was once a heavily-manned installation is now operating on a skeleton crew. Although they have no official designation, they are unofficially known as the Zeta Team. At any given time, the military portion of the team consists of six people. This brings the entire population of the planetoid up to nine."

That number destroyed any last hope that there was some positive way for Marco to look at his assignment. With only nine people on the entire rock, there was no way this wasn't the most tedious assignment in history. And yet, he was sure that Colonel Horitz was about to say something to make it even worse.

"Because of the top secret nature of the installation, there is no regular rotation of people in and out of Zeta Team. Those who are assigned here are not able to leave at all until they finish their service with the Interplanetary Army. Given the amount of time you have already put in, Marco, I'm sure you can do the math."

He could. It meant that the earliest he could possibly leave this place was in two and a half Earth-Standard years. Two and a half years, only eight other people, and a planetoid so lifeless that it had never even been assigned a proper name.

"I'm sorry Marco," Horitz said. "I really am. But I still believe there's a place for you here. In fact, I know it. This is where you can prove yourself. So I wish you good luck, soldier."

The holo-message stopped, leaving only the dead-looking planetoid to fill up the screen.

3

Up until the moment the ship landed and Marco walked down the boarding ramp, he tried to keep up his hopes that this couldn't possibly be as bad as it all sounded.

It was.

The first problem was that it appeared to be nighttime on this particular patch of 54174340. That wouldn't have been such a big deal if he couldn't clearly see the sun in the sky. Marco asked the shipboard AI about this before he went to the ramp, to which vIdI replied that, not only was the atmosphere thin enough that the sky never became more than a dull purple when the local star was at its highest, but that the star's Class D status meant it wasn't big enough to provide the standard amount of light he was used to on other worlds. The planetoid might rotate like any other world, but it would never have a full day. The best he could hope for was a dull twilight.

The second problem was that there was no one around to meet him. In fact, there wasn't anything at all. The ship's landing zone was on a rocky gray plain, although it couldn't exactly be called flat. The planetoid was so small that Marco could see a slight curve on the horizon. And yet, despite that, he didn't see any buildings or man-made structures anywhere in his sight.

"Hey!" Marco called back up the ramp, although the pilot was nowhere in sight. vIdI had been a better conversationalist, and it only had a simulated personality. "Hey, is someone going to escort me to where I need to go?"

"You're already where you need to go!" the pilot called back from somewhere.

"I mean, where's the barracks? Or isn't there going to be someone coming to meet me?"

"No one ever bothers to come to the landing zone unless they've been told we have a supply shipment," the pilot yelled. "As for where you should go, just follow the lightning. You'll get there eventually. Now if you don't mind, could you please get off the boarding ramp so I can fricking get out of this place?"

Marco stepped away from the boarding ramp. The instant he was a safe distance away, the ramp pulled back up and the engines whirred for takeoff. It was in the air and heading back to the core worlds before Marco could think of any other questions he might ask.

Okay. So. His first moments on 54174340 were less than welcoming. He wouldn't let any of this drive him down, though. He was still a representative of the Interplanetary Army. Marco would continue to conduct himself as such, even as he had to slog across a barren world to get to, uh, wherever exactly it was he was supposed to go now.

He stood at the landing zone for nearly a minute before he saw something light the sky from some distance away. It had been brief, so quick that he almost hadn't seen it, but as with so many other things, that short flash was all he needed to burn the image into his brain. That would be the static discharge he'd been told about, which meant that the ruins, and likely the barracks, were that way.

With his rucksack and his rifle slung on his shoulders, Marco started in that direction and found that the simple act of moving improved his mood. Colonel Horitz had said he'd believed in Marco, that he thought Marco had something he could honestly contribute here. While Marco supposed that could have just been a lie designed to make Marco more accepting of what he now realized was probably the worst assignment in all of the Interplanetary Army, Marco didn't think Horitz would be false with him. At least not about something like this. Horitz had always done right by Marco during his teen years, and Marco had no doubt that, to Horitz, he was the son the colonel had never had. Marco wanted to follow in Horitz's footsteps, and Horitz wanted Marco to find his niche in the universe. If Horitz somehow thought Marco could find it on this backwater, then Marco trusted him.

And besides, Marco reasoned, there were only eight other people on this planet. Someone new had to be a momentous occasion to them. He was sure that, when he finally found someone, they would give him a perfect, wonderful greeting.

Two structures quickly appeared on the horizon, with a third jumbled form just beyond. While the third resisted easy categorization, Marco could tell immediately what the other two buildings were. One was a barracks, the pre-fab kind that the Interplanetary Army could set up quickly yet would still be strong enough to hold against a couple of low-level missile blasts. It looked significantly larger than needed for a force that supposedly consisted of nothing more than six people, so Marco assumed it was a holdover from the days when 54174340 had actually been considered of some military importance. The other building was equally pre-fab but of a decidedly different design. The walls around it were plain white, but it had a number of dura-glass domes sticking out of it in odd places like the place had developed the universe's most bizarre case of acne. This would have to be the facility used by the scientists. It was larger than the barracks, yet with only three people in it Marco figured that it too had a lot of empty space inside.

It was just outside this building that Marco saw his first resident of 54174340. The woman wore a worn yet clean jumpsuit. While the suit was hardly what anyone would consider sexy, Marco, being the healthy young straight man that he was, immediately noticed the way it fit a little too snuggly around her chest. She had long, unkempt black hair and dirty glasses, which she took off her face and tried to polish on her jumpsuit as she paced back and forth in front of the building's entrance. While Marco immediately found something attractive about her, he swore to himself that he would conduct himself professionally and never, at any point, make any advances on her. He was a representative of the army, after all, and he would conduct himself like it.

When he got close enough to her, he attempted to introduce himself. "Hi. I'm Private Marco Cruz. I'm looking for…"

"Oh, perfect! Yes, yes!" the woman called out as she saw him. Before he could do anything else, she ran up to him and pulled out, of all things, a tape measure. It wasn't even a holo-tape measure, but an actual, physical tape measure like Marco might see in a museum. "It's about time. Stand still. I'm going to need all your measurements."

Marco stood still, too confused by her behavior to respond, as she used the measure to get his height, the width of his waist, his in-seam, his arm span, and the height of his ear. It wasn't until she started measuring his nostrils that he tried to step away.

"I'm sorry, but I don't understand this," Marco said. "Why are you taking these measurements?"

"For my *data*," she said, as though he had to be a complete idiot to not have already known this. "Now, for the really important measurements. Drop your pants."

"Wait, what? Why?"

"Because I need to measure your member. I need both length and girth, and I need these measurements in all its states."

She started to reach for his belt buckle, but he stepped away. "No!"

That word stopped her cold, freezing her in place as though she was afraid to make another move.

"Doc! Damn it, I told you before, I wanted to talk to the new kid before you got to him!"

Both of them turned to look at the new voice. Another woman was approaching from the direction of the barracks, and Marco didn't think it was possible for the two women to look any more different from each other. While the first woman was obviously one of the three civilian scientists, this new one was military, and held herself like an officer. Marco immediately stood at attention. He had no doubt that he was now in the presence of the senior-most ranking person on the planetoid. Even the first woman clearly deferred to her.

"I know what you said," the first woman said. "But it's highly important for my research that I make my observations as close to planet fall for new personnel as possible. If I don't…"

"If you don't, that just means you'll have a half hour difference. Given the nature of your 'research,' as you call it, I don't think half an hour will make that much of a difference."

The first woman blushed, making Marco all the more curious as to what her research actually entailed. "Yes, major. I understand. I trust that you will send the specimen to me as soon as you're done with him?"

"Doc, I've told you repeatedly. Stop referring to the people under my command as specimens."

The look she gave the major suggested that she didn't know what else she could possibly be expected to call them, but at last she nodded and went back to the science building. Marco stayed at attention while the major looked him up and down. Although she was short, she had broad shoulders and the kind of physique that could only come from constant workouts. Her hair was cut very short, and she had a lit cigar in her hand. The name on her uniform said Stonewerth.

"At ease, soldier," the major finally said.

Marco took up a rest position. Major Stonewerth shook her head and smiled.

"No, really, Private Cruz. At ease."

Marco gave her a confused look. "I'm sorry, I don't understand. I am at ease."

Stonewerth barked a laugh. "Oh, I do so love the new ones," she said to no one in particular. "Soldier, if you were back on your home world, and you were standing at a crosswalk waiting for the light to say you could go, how would you stand?"

"Sir, I would stand exactly like this."

Stonewerth looked him up and down again. "Really?"

"Yes, sir. Really."

"Stop calling me sir."

"Yes, ma'am."

"None of that, either. You don't even need to call me major. Doc over there is the only one who still calls me that, even though I've repeatedly told her not to. If you have to act semi-formal with me, you may call me Stonewerth. Otherwise everyone around here just calls me Stone."

"Yes m... uh, yes, Stonewerth."

"Oh boy," Stonewerth said. "You're going to be a doozy." She slowly walked around him, taking in every detail. Her cigar smoke wafted into his nose, making it hard for him to maintain his composure. "I received your file ahead of your arrival, of course. I have to say it surprised me."

"And why is that m... Stonewerth?"

"In case you haven't already guessed by the information you should have been given during your initial briefing, we don't get the best of the best sent to us. We get the screw-ups, the has-beens, the ones that have no right to be in the Interplanetary Army yet have nowhere else to go. Would you say that describes you,

Cruz?"

Marco gulped back the bitter retort he wished he could deliver. "That's what I've been told."

"And yet, just by looking at you, you look perfect. You appear to be the poster boy for the model soldier. It's not until someone looks deeper into your file that they see why you'd get sent here." Stonewerth stopped in front of him again and looked him in the eye. "I have to say I'm especially impressed by the incident on Carmen. Did you *really* think that woman's hat was a bomb?"

Marco tried to answer without a hitch in his voice. "It contained all the materials needed to make a rudimentary explosive."

"Yes, I'm sure it did. Just like I'm sure it also contained all the materials to make a rudimentary hat. You're damned lucky her hair eventually grew back."

Marco couldn't disagree with that.

"Tell me something, Cruz. What did you expect was going to happen when you got this assignment?"

"I expected I had one last chance to prove myself."

"And now, given what you were probably told on the ship and what you've seen so far during your stay on our lovely little planetoid, what do you expect is going to happen instead?"

"I expect I have one last chance to prove myself."

Stonewerth let loose a great, echoing guffaw. "Oh, that's great. That's exactly the kind of attitude a member of the Interplanetary Army should have. Too bad it's going to be completely and utterly wasted here. It's going to be a terrible shame watching that attitude get slowly leached out of you." Her voice took on a distinctly melancholy tone at the end. "Well, I suppose we best get going with your 'orientation.'" Marco could practically hear the quotation marks around that last word. "We'll head back to the barracks and you can meet the rest of the team."

Stonewerth led the way to the barracks. Cruz started to follow, but his head quickly snapped to the side as the ruins emitted another static charge high into the air before it disappeared into space. Stonewerth stopped and gestured for him to follow.

"Don't worry. You can see the ruins later. In fact, you're going to be seeing a lot of the stupid things for the next few years, so I wouldn't be in any hurry if I were you."

Marco followed, but he continued to look at the ruins along the way. He replayed that flash in his memory, over and over, and thinking about what he had thought he'd seen. It was lunacy, not possible, and no one would believe him. Yet he still remembered, and made a note to be out here to watch the static flashes whenever possible.

4

It was a typical barracks, just like practically every other one he had ever seen, just with one major difference: given that there were only six people who lived here, most of the nearly one hundred beds had been shoved aside and stacked out of the way. In their place someone had painted white lines and geometric patterns on the floor. He realized immediately that this was some kind of court for a sport, but he had no clue for which one. This took up the front portion of the barracks. In the back were the few remaining unmolested beds, along with a bunch of structures that had been jury-rigged from bed pieces. Some of them were probably supposed to be couches and chairs, while Marco's best guess was that the rest were intended as exercise equipment. Whatever they were supposed to be, Marco could count sixty-eight clear and separate code violations in just his first few seconds in the barracks. He decided to stop counting, since there would probably be far more where those had come from.

"Welcome to the Hall," Stonewerth said as she led him through the sports court. "Yeah, I know it's not that imaginative of a name, but it had that name before I got here, so don't blame me. Right now you're standing in the Sportsball court."

"What sport do you play here?"

"Uh, Sportsball."

"Sportsball isn't a real sport."

"That doesn't stop us from playing it. I'd try to explain the rules to you, but no one actually knows what they are. Over there is the exercise and weight area, obviously, and then the spot we call the living room. Yes, yes, I know. We can't really call it a room when it doesn't have any walls, but that's hardly the most egregious rule that gets broken around here. Beyond that are the beds, and the toilet and showers beyond that. That door over there goes to the mess hall, but I wouldn't go in there right now. It's a mess."

Marco looked at her face to see if this had been intended as a joke, but if it was, she'd told it so many times that even she was bored with it.

"This... this all seems highly non-standard," Marco said.

"You ain't seen nothing yet, kid. You still need to meet the rest of the team." Stonewerth stopped and looked like a thought had suddenly occurred to her. "Hey, Cruz, you wouldn't happen to be gay, would you?"

"Huh? Um, no, I'm not."

"Bisexual? Pansexual? Maxisexual?"

"Not that I'm aware of, although I have to confess I don't actually know what that last one is."

"Huh. That's too bad. Not for you, but for Spam. That poor guy just can't seem to get a break. Stop giving me that look, Cruz, you'll understand why I'm asking in a minute, after I introduce you to everyone."

Stonewerth whistled. "Hey! A-tennnnnn-shun! Everyone report to meet the new guy!"

Previously Marco hadn't noticed anyone else in the Hall with them, which was quite the feat considering the way he'd already been committing every single detail to memory. Someone rolled out from under one of the beds and stumbled to his feet. Two women that looked uncannily alike came out of the mess. The last member of the team unfolded himself from where he'd been lying on a couch that had been facing away. Given his colossal height and gangly limbs, Marco wasn't sure how he'd managed to sit on the couch without anything sticking out over the edge.

The four other members of Zeta Team lined up along what Marco assumed was some kind of foul line or free-throw line on the floor. He stood at attention for several seconds before he realized that he was the only person in the entire room that was doing so. Reluctantly, Marco slouched a little, not liking the way it made him feel.

"Okay, okay, okay," Stonewerth said as she paced between Marco and the rest of the crew. "Everyone introduce yourselves. New guy, you go first."

"Private first class Marco Cruz, reporting for duty," Marco said. He wasn't sure this was quite the right time for that line, but something told him he wouldn't be using it at any other time, and the little bit of formality set him at ease.

The four other members all looked at him with a spectrum of emotions ranging from incredulity to amusement. Marco tried to ignore it, and instead read the names on their uniforms. Verde, Murphy, Murphy, and Odwall. Marco would have expected them to introduce themselves as such, but he was wrong.

Verde, the first one in line, raised his hand and gave Marco a little wave. "Spam," he said. Marco would have thought he was offering him lunchmeat if he hadn't already heard the name from Stonewerth. He was a medium sized man with mocha-colored skin and a pencil-thin mustache. Spam looked at Marco hesitantly and expectantly, an expression that faded away when Stonewerth shook her head at him.

"Sorry, Spam, I already asked. That's not how he swings."

Spam nodded. Marco had to fight to ask Stonewerth what kind of group she was running here, if she thought part of her duty was to play matchmaker with her soldiers.

The woman that was next in line, the first with the nametag of Murphy, gave Marco an exaggerated wave that reminded him of some extremely old show that he thought even pre-dated holo-vids. He struggled for a moment to remember the name. Oh, right. *The Mickey Mouse Club*. This woman said hi like she was one of the Mouseketeers.

"Tulip!" she said, and while Marco was sure that it was a nickname, not her real name, he didn't think he'd ever seen someone fit their name so well. Her brown hair was a decidedly un-army-like length, but that wasn't nearly as much of a break from regulations as the patchwork flowers and butterflies that she had sewn at random places all over her uniform.

The woman next to her with the same last name had facial features so remarkably like Tulip that they could only be either clones or twins. Marco guessed probably the latter, since neither of them looked old enough to be part of the last generation of legal clones, and he doubted they would have been able to fake that particular genetic test well enough to get into the Interplanetary Army. Or maybe they had, and when it had been discovered, the army had decided to cover them up by sending them here. Marco had heard rumors of such things, but had never thought they could be true.

Whether twins or clones, though, their facial and body structure was where the similarities ended. This one's hair was buzzed close, closer than it needed to be for a female soldier, as though she were trying to make up for the blatant rule-flaunting of the other Murphy. Her uniform was completely according to regulations, and she scowled at her twin like she couldn't possibly understand how or why anyone would be that happy.

"Thorn," the woman said. No, apparently Marco had been wrong in thinking that it wasn't possible for anyone's name to suit them better than Tulip. This woman looked *exactly* like she should be called Thorn.

The last person in line towered over all the others to the point that Marco had to wonder how his skeleton could even support him. He was incredibly thin, had pale skin, and a shaved head. His most striking feature, though, was the mask that covered the lower half of his face. It was black and looked custom made, with a port in the front that looked like maybe it might hook up to some kind of feeding tube. Did this guy really not even take the mask off to eat?

Marco waited several seconds for him to say his name. When the man did nothing, Marco tried to prompt him. "And you are…?"

The man shrugged.

"Uh…" Marco said.

Stonewerth laughed. "No, that's actually his name. Or at least that's what we call him, since that's usually how he answers everything. Say hi, Shrug."

Shrug waved.

"Aaaaand that's about as formal as we get around here," Stonewerth said. "Everyone, you can go back to your business. I've got to keep orienting the new guy to our particular brand of weirdness."

"Wait, that's it?" Marco asked Stonewerth as the others wandered back to whatever they had been doing.

"That's it," Stonewerth said. "I've still got to take you over to the Complex so you can meet the science crew, although you've already met Doc."

"Um, yeah, what was that about?"

"Walk with me and I'll explain how things work around here, Cruz. I'm going to call you Cruz for now, but don't expect to be called that for long. Except for me sometimes, no one ever gets called by their legal names."

Stonewerth led Cruz back out of the Hall, where they stood just outside the door.

"This place isn't even close to what I expected," Marco said.

"Let me guess. No one actually told you exactly where you were being sent until after you woke from stasis, right?"

"That's right."

"And when you were told, you got the standard spiel about how this is all supposed to be a secret even though it's now just a skeleton crew?"

"Yes, that's correct."

"What you probably weren't told is that no one actually expects the mystery of the ruins to be deciphered anymore. Shithead is where they send the troops that are too much of an embarrassment to be anywhere else, and where they put the scientists that no one actually trusts with scientific equipment anymore."

"Wait, Shithead?"

"That's what we call the planetoid. Take the numbers of 54174340 and turn them into their closest approximation in capital letters, and it becomes SHITHEAD. Welcome to Planet Shithead, the most God-forsaken place in the known universe."

"You almost make it sound like a prison," Marco said.

"I hate to break it to you, kid, but that's more or less where we are. A prison for those the IPA needs to get rid of but haven't actually committed a crime. And until your term of service is up, you're stuck here."

5

"I'm sure you've figured it out already, but protocol is a little relaxed here," Stonewerth said as she slowly walked Marco toward the science building, what she had referred to as the Complex.

"I thought it might be before I got off the ship," Marco said, "but I have to say I'm shocked at how far you've let things go beyond regulations. Uh, if I'm allowed to voice that opinion to you, that is."

"You are, and go right ahead," Stonewerth said. She stopped in the middle of the worn footpath between the two buildings and did a deep knee bend. It was only then that Marco heard the subtle sound of servos working in her leg. Stonewerth was a cyborg, and had likely lost her leg in a battle. That alone shouldn't have been enough for the Interplanetary Army to toss her aside, but it probably hadn't helped her situation.

"Sorry," Stonewerth said. "If I don't do that every so often it has a tendency to lock up. They send replacement parts sometimes with the supply ships, but never enough. I've got to do what I can to keep it functioning."

After a few more bends she stood straight and gestured for Marco to follow her again. "As I said, you go ahead and voice your opinion. Simply by being here, you're in a shitty situation and you're not going to get out of it. The last thing you or any other member of the Zeta Team needs is for me to remove some way for you to blow off steam. If I didn't let everyone have less than savory opinions once in a while, they might take out their frustrations in more un-healthy ways."

"Is that something you've had a problem with before?" Marco asked.

Stonewerth stopped again and turned to him with a decidedly dark look on her face. "Yes, we have. And it's actually fortunate that you brought it up, because we need to go over the single most important rule I have here. I might let all of you get away with things the army wouldn't allow elsewhere, but this one rule is law. That's the reason there was a place for you here. The last person in your place got it in her head that this rule didn't apply to her, so now she's not here anymore. Do you want to know what that rule is?"

"Yes."

"No."

Marco blinked. "Uh, no as in you won't tell me, or no as in…"

"No as in that's the rule. No means no. For anything. Period. People do a lot of not-so regulation activities around here to keep themselves from going stir-crazy, if you know what I mean, but if you or anyone else says that no, you don't want in on something that's not directly related to your obligatory duties, then you drop it. Immediately."

"You mean, like that Sportsball game you were talking about?" Marco asked. "If the others try to make me play, and I don't want to, they can't force me?"

"I… what?" Stonewerth said. "Kid, sure, I guess that would apply too, but please tell me they didn't send someone so naïve that you really don't get what I'm talking about."

Marco remembered the moment earlier when the woman, Doc, had been reaching for his pants, and the way she had completely frozen in place when Marco had said the magic word. "Oh," Marco finally said. "You mean…"

"There's nine people on this entire planetoid. Per IPA regulations, all of them are fitted with fertility dampeners and aggressive long-release anti-virals. Beyond that, all we have to occupy our time is a made-up sport, a small library of holo-vids, a workout area, and whatever the hell it is the scientists do to keep themselves occupied deep within the Complex. So yes, to say it straight out, people around here screw like bunnies."

"I see," Marco said tentatively. "I'm certainly not completely inexperienced in that, but I'm not sure if…"

"That's fine. You don't want to participate, then you don't. If you do, then just ask around and you can find out the dynamics of who likes what pretty easily. But consent is the law here, period."

"And what happens if someone disobeys that law?" Marco asked.

Marco hadn't thought it was possible for Stonewerth's face to get any more serious, but it did. "Then that person ends up like

Robinson."

"Robinson?" Marco asked. "Is that the person I'm replacing?"

"Yes."

"What happened to her?"

"Tell me something, Cruz. Do you see any prison or jail cells around here?"

"Not that I've seen yet."

"And how long do you think it takes for a ship to be dispatched to here if we don't want someone around anymore?"

"Quite a long time, I'd guess."

"Right. So what do you *think* happened to Robinson?"

Marco thought about it. He didn't have to think about it for long. "I understand."

"Good," Stonewerth said, some of the levity returning to her voice. "As long as you get that, we'll all get along swimmingly. So let's introduce you to the rest of the science nerds, and then I can show you the ruins."

The first room inside the Complex looked like it had once been intended as a reception area, complete with a desk for a secretary and a waiting room. The desk looked lonely and dusty, while the waiting room now seemed to be a storage area for various junk.

"We don't throw anything away around here," Stonewerth said, pointing at the haphazard piles. "Given how long it takes to get materials and placement parts, everyone gets pretty adept at jury-rigging things they need with whatever we have lying around."

Down the hall from there Stonewerth showed him a room that was probably supposed to be some kind of laboratory. It didn't look much different than the waiting room except for the older, mustachioed man puttering around inside. "Hey, Weirdlust!" Stonewerth called to him. "Did you want to meet the new guy?"

The man looked up from whatever he was doing long enough to give a half-hearted wave. "Hello. Your name?"

"Marco Cruz."

Weirdlust cocked his head as though that was the strangest name he'd ever heard, then looked at Stonewerth questioningly.

"He hasn't earned a nickname yet," Stonewerth said. "Give

him a few days."

Weirdlust nodded. "Have you warned him about Doc yet?"

"He already met her on the way in."

"Did she try to measure his member?"

"Yep."

Weirdlust looked back at Marco. "Her reasons for that are more innocent than you think. For that, at least. Remember, if you don't want to participate in anything with her, you can always…"

"Say no," Marco said. "Yeah, Stonewerth already gave me that speech."

"Cool. See you around, then." Weirdlust bent back to his work, which Marco now saw consisted of measuring a bunch of gray rocks.

Once they were out of the old man's earshot down the hallway, Marco asked Stonewerth, "Weirdlust?"

"Yeah, you know, like that old holo, *Dr. Strangelove*, except not like that at all. Don't ask me where that particular nickname came from. I think my predecessor who gave it to him was drunk at the time. He's odd, just like the other two scientists. Hell, if one manages to get stuck on this planet it's already pretty much guaranteed that you're pretty strange. But he's a little more personable than Doc. He's also one of the reasons I was hoping to maybe play matchmaker with you and Spam. Weirdlust is the only other guy on the planet with any interest in other guys, meaning that while the rest of us have a few options regarding who we can spend some nights with, Weirdlust is Spam's only option. And while Spam won't kiss and tell, Tulip says Weirdlust is pretty bland in the sack."

"Is that seriously something people talk about around here?"

"Wow, kid, you really must have lived a sheltered life."

They passed another set of labs that looked pretty abandoned, then found their way into some kind of kitchen. Here Marco saw a familiar face. Doc was on her knees in front of an open refrigerator, a surgical mask on her face and heavy rubber gloves on her hands. She had a long pair of tongs, which she used to gingerly pull out something that was a disturbing greenish-gray color.

"Doc, how many times have I told you not to do your

experiments in the public refrigerator?" Stonewerth said. "You've got your own cooling unit for those kinds of things."

"I'm not doing an experiment," Doc said testily. She didn't even bother to look in Stonewerth's direction. "I'm just cleaning out the fridge."

"You never clean out the fridge unless you've released something virulent in it again."

"Okay, fine. I'm cleaning out one of my samples that escaped from its Petri dish."

"Damn it, Doc. If you give Hamlet a bacterial infection again…"

"I'm not. Trust me."

Stonewerth mumbled something under her breath about trusting Doc on the day aliens invaded the planetoid and made them all wear funny hats. Despite himself, Marco had to smile as they left the kitchen.

"So I'm assuming that Hamlet is the last scientist?" Marco asked.

"Yep. And in order to meet him, we'll probably have to go over to the last stop on our sight-seeing tour. He's the only person on Shithead that still takes the idea of deciphering the ruins seriously."

Once they were back outside, it was only a short walk to the alien ruins. When Marco had first heard of the ruins while on the ship, he'd pictured something enormous and cyclopean, a monument to a lost race that would be full of mystery and wonder.

Instead he got a pile of stones.

"Well, that's underwhelming," Marco said.

"Yep," Stonewerth said. "This is why we're here on the ass end of the galaxy, for a bunch of blocks that look like they were knocked over by a giant child."

To be fair, they were at least an *interesting* pile of stones. They'd been carved into various geometric shapes that clearly had not been caused by nature, and the closer Marco got to them the more he felt a static hum in the air. Most fascinating of all, though, was the fact that some of them were glowing. The glowing ones all had some kind of intricate symbols written on all sides, with the symbols themselves providing the majority of the light. As he watched, the glowing faded and the symbols disappeared.

"Whoops. Better back up," Stonewerth said as she took a few steps away from the stones.

"Why?" Marco asked. "Is something going to…"

Lightning cracked the air directly over the stones. Marco was actually thrown back off his feet from the concussion wave. When he stood back up, Stonewerth was standing next to him and shaking her head. "I told you."

"The electrical discharge," Marco said. "I'm guessing that it happens when the symbols disappear."

"Yep. Now the symbols are going to slowly start to appear on a bunch of completely different stones."

"The most interesting thing is that there doesn't seem to be any pattern," someone else said. Marco looked over to see a man that he could only assume was Hamlet. He was the youngest of the three scientists, and for possibly related reasons, he looked to be the least worn or wild-eyed. "The timing is always different, which stones glow is always different, hell, even the symbols that appear on each stone change. There are deep archives in the Complex with nearly a century's worth of data, and none of the AI programs we set to study them can ever make sense of any of it."

"Then again, it's not like anyone's been making much of an effort to decode it all," Stonewerth said.

"Yes, I've gathered that," Hamlet said with a frown. "I don't like saying it, but I think my two colleagues became quite cracked long before I got here. It kind of makes me wonder how long before the same thing happens to me."

Stonewerth looked at Marco. "Hamlet here was the resident new guy before you showed up."

"How long have you been here?" Marco asked Hamlet.

"About six Earth-standard months. Given the speed at which 54174340 orbits its sun, that would be just over four years according to local time."

"It's best not to think of it in those terms, though," Stonewerth said. "That's only going to make you go nutty quicker. We still use Earth-standard time for everything just to make it easier on everyone."

"You make it sound like it's a foregone conclusion that I'm

going to have some kind of breakdown," Marco said.

"That's because it is, Cruz. It happens to everyone. It might be a small mental break, it might be a big one. Your personality might just change to make you more grouchy, or one day you could wake up and be completely convinced that you're Joan of Arc."

"Speaking of that, how's Tulip been doing?" Hamlet asked.

"Better," Stonewerth said. "Almost back to her disgustingly cheery self, mostly thanks to her sister, I think. At the very least, she's no longer afraid one of us is going to burn her at the stake."

"Please tell me you're both kidding," Marco asked.

"Maybe we are, maybe we aren't," Stonewerth said. "But the point is true either way. We're all stuck out here, kid. There's not going to be a change to the monotony. You're going to be pushed to your mental limits here, so the important thing to remember is that everyone on Zeta Team is family. Whether we want to be or not."

Marco turned to stare at the ruins as Hamlet kept talking. "You know, I've always wondered, why are we all called the Zeta Team?"

"Probably just because they needed a pretentious sounding name that wouldn't scare the newcomers off," Stonewerth said. "But personally, I think that maybe it's because we're not their A team. We're not even their B team. We're so far down their list that they ran out of Arabic letters and had to stick us near the end of the Greek alphabet instead."

Marco's mind raced with all of this. He was stuck here now, and he wasn't sure what to do with it all.

The symbols on the stones pulsed, slowly getting brighter and building up the static in the air again.

6

The next twenty-seven days somehow managed to be both the strangest and most boring days of Marco's life.

The rest of that first day consisted of him claiming a bed in the Hall and then calmly cataloguing the idiosyncrasies of his new squad mates. Although he didn't play himself, Marco watched his first game of Sportsball. Even for someone as detail oriented as Marco, the rules were completely incomprehensible. He got the feeling that was perfectly fine, however, as no one else seemed to know what the rules were either. The only consistent aspect of the game was that it was played with a hastily stitched-together ball made of a pillowcase filled with something that might have been rice. It was a wonder the ball never split and revealed its contents, given how hard the players hit it and threw it and kicked it and batted it and bounced it and smashed it. There might have been some kind of goal at either side of the Sportsball court, but no one seemed to agree on its boundaries, nor did anyone seem to care. If someone declared that they had scored, then they did. If someone said there was a foul, then there was. If someone decided that it was now time to drop the ball in the center of the court and beat it repeatedly with sticks, then everyone joined in until someone randomly declared a winner.

On the second day, Marco learned that Zeta Team's definition of "training" and "keeping in shape" were pretty suspect. There were rifles and a weapons range out behind the Hall, but while they were allowed to aim at the makeshift targets all they wanted, they couldn't actually fire. Bullets were at a premium here, Stonewerth explained, and they couldn't afford to waste them simply for target practice. When Marco asked what they were saving the ammunition for, Stonewerth simply shrugged and said, "I don't know. Maybe command thinks the aliens will eventually come back and we'll need to save the galaxy from them."

On the third day, Marco realized that most of the other people on Planetoid Shithead (despite himself, he'd already started calling it that in his head) were giving him strange looks and stares. When he finally asked Stonewerth about it, she simply said, "They want to screw you."

"I... wait, huh?"

"I told you on your first day that everyone has a tendency to get frisky with each other," Stonewerth said.

"Isn't that kind of fraternization supposed to be against regulations?"

"Of course. But it's funny that you still seem to think that matters around here."

Although Marco didn't feel like he was ready yet to "get frisky" with some of these people, he asked Stonewerth about the dynamics of how such things worked around here. Apparently, no one on Zeta Team had any real concept of a significant other or monogamy. If a person was interested in sleeping with someone, that person asked them. If they said no, then you went on to the next candidate. Spam was gay, Weirdlust and Thorn considered themselves bisexual, and everyone else was more-or-less straight. The "more-or-less" part came from the fact that people tended to eventually get bored with the same couple of people over and over, so they were prone to experimentation.

Stonewerth explained all this to Marco while they were together in Marco's bed.

"I'm not sure how comfortable I am with sleeping with my commanding officer," Marco told her when they were finished.

"You'll get over it eventually," Stonewerth told him. "Around here, sex doesn't tend to be anything more than a diversion. In fact, depending on what people are currently using as the rules in Sportsball, it might not even be the most interesting or intimate thing you do with the other people around you."

On the fourth day, Marco played Sportsball for the first time. On the fifth day, he spent the day recovering from his injuries in bed. He had to admit, Stonewerth was right. Sportsball could get far more interesting than sex. That didn't stop him from spending a small portion of that bed day with Tulip.

On the sixth day, Marco felt incredibly guilty about how much he had been slacking, and therefore spent the majority of the day in training. Spam joined him during aiming practice, and Marco had his first somewhat meaningful conversation with someone other than Stonewerth.

"How've you been adjusting?" Spam asked as they both lined up their rifles and mimicked firing. Marco had to admit the practice left a little bit to be desired.

"I'm still getting used to this place," Marco said. "I'm still not entirely sure what to think of it all."

"There's not really much *to* think about it," Spam said.

"Hey, do you mind if I asked how you got saddled with a name like Spam?"

"It's a joke regarding how I ended up getting sent here." Spam stopped aiming his gun, instead opting to sit on a nearby rock and polish the rifle with a rag. The rag was so greasy that it probably put more dirt on the weapon than it took off. "See, my home world is Lewis-and-Clark. Ever hear of it?"

"Yeah. I'd be surprised if someone hadn't. Because of the... well, you know."

"Yep, I do know. Poor civic planning when it was colonized led to massive food shortages. Which, unfortunately, led to the cannibalism that everyone associates with the planet. And no, because everyone just *has* to ask, I've never eaten human flesh. That doesn't actually happen that often. It's sensationalized garbage."

"But the food shortages?"

"Not sensationalized. Those are real. And I got sent here because I decided to take a less-than-sanctioned approach to fix it."

"Wait," Marco lowered his weapon and stared at Spam in amazement. He'd been living the past five days with a famous political figure and he hadn't even realized it. "Is your first name Simon? Are you *the* Simon Verde?"

"In the flesh."

"As in, the Robin Hood of the Outer Colonial Worlds?"

"Oh God. Please tell me they're not still calling me that?"

"They are."

"Damn. Well, whatever stories you've heard, they're probably just as exaggerated as the stories of cannibalism. I simply found some extra food and sent it to my home world."

"So you didn't steal two billion military rations?"

"No, I did that. Although I don't like to call it stealing. I simply changed a few ones and zeroes in the requisition files. Instead of sitting in a warehouse slowly going bad, they ended up where they could do the most good. The IPA needed to punish me, but outright booting me out of the military would be bad publicity, what with all the images in the newsfeeds of starving children finally being able to eat. So here I am."

"I still don't get why you're called Spam," Marco said.

Spam shrugged. "Most of the food was processed meat."

"It's an unfortunate name to get stuck with."

"You should talk. Are you aware that if you don't show some other personality trait soon, you're going to get stuck with the name Stick?"

"Why Stick?"

"You're going to get named after that stick you've got up your butt."

Marco chose to ignore that for now. It wasn't exactly a name he wanted to get stuck with, but it was still better than Spam. "What about everyone else?" Marco asked. "How'd they get their names?"

"Well, Stone is obvious. Weirdlust, no one knows, not even him. I've actually heard him wondering aloud about the origins of his name in his sleep, if you can believe it. Hamlet's is pretty innocuous. He brought an old-school physical copy of Shakespeare with him when he came. Doc, well, I'm not sure that any of us actually know what her real name is supposed to be. She's just got a doctorate of some sort, and that's what she calls herself."

"What about Tulip and Thorn?"

Spam laughed. "Oh, that one's rich. Would you believe that Tulip and Thorn's actual names are Thorn and Tulip?"

"Really?"

"Their parents apparently got it in their heads that they wanted to name their twin daughters something that would fit their temperaments. So they waited a few months after they were born to give them their official names. One was sweet and cuddly and loveable, while the other one threw a fit all the time. So, Tulip and Thorn. Then, after a few months, they started to switch up their personalities. Tulip got surly, and Thorn became the giggly baby.

And those were the traits that stuck with them. They're the only ones here that picked their own nicknames. They both agreed that the other's name was more appropriate for them, so Thorn and Tulip became Tulip and Thorn. And don't you ever go mixing the names up, either. Tulip will just get pouty about it, but Thorn will legitimately kick your ass. And then, obviously, there's Shrug. He's kind of self-explanatory."

"Not really. Why doesn't he talk?"

"Ask him to show you what's beneath that mask of his sometime. You'll see." Spam stood up. "I'm heading back inside." He paused for a moment before asking. "Hey, are you sure you aren't up for a little, uh, 'experimenting' with me?"

"Sorry," Marco said. "Not really my thing."

"Hey, can't blame a guy for trying."

On the seventh day, as it became more and more obvious that no one around here would adhere to the fixed military schedule Marco had lived his life by ever since meeting Horitz, Marco wandered off to the ruins. He spent most of the day staring at them, memorizing the glowing symbols and backing away only when another blast of electricity was imminent. He was starting to develop some thoughts on the mysterious artifacts, but he needed more details before he felt comfortable sharing any of them.

On the eighth day, Marco did in fact end up experimenting, but not with Spam. That was apparently what Doc always called it whenever she ended up in bed with someone. Not only did she actually measure his private parts beforehand, but she stopped frequently during the act to take notes. When they were done, she declared the experiment inconclusive and resolved to do it over again repeatedly until she was happy with the results. Marco told her he wasn't sure he was willing to do that. The whole experience had kind of freaked him out.

Days nine through nineteen blurred together in his mind, which was quite impressive for someone with his knack for memory and details. He spent lots of time at the ruins just staring at them, which finally earned him his nickname: Glare. Marco accepted it. At least it was better than Stick. He continued to keep up with the IPA standards he had embraced before coming here even when no one else did. Thorn made fun of him for that, Tulip thought it was cute, and Stonewerth just watched him intently as he meticulously cleaned his gear and made his bed as though this were just another assignment, exactly as important as any other. He shared his bed with Thorn, and then Stonewerth again, although he still felt guilty about it. He played Sportsball, and even won a couple of games. Or at least he thought he did. It wasn't really clear if the game even had a winner or a loser.

On day twenty he got very depressed for no apparent reason. Everyone else gave him a wide berth that day, except for Tulip, who left him little origami flowers next to his dinner plate in an effort to cheer him up. Later on, before the two of them went to sleep next to each other, she explained that it happened to everyone here. Planetoid Shithead just had that sort of effect on people, and they all dealt with it in their own ways.

As if to illustrate this, Tulip had a relapse of her Joan of Arc fantasy on the morning of day twenty-one. The rest of the team walked Marco through how to help bring her down, which turned out to be a complex combination of indulging her fantasy and subtly reminding her that she was not, in fact, in Medieval France. By the end of the day she seemed more or less back to normal, but Marco had trouble sleeping that night, wondering if those were the kind of mental breaks he would see often around here, and how prone he himself would be to them.

He spent all of day twenty-two staring at the ruins, not talking to anyone. On day twenty-three he finally went up to Shrug and asked to see what was under the mask. Shrug obliged, showing Marco the scarred ruin that was the bottom of his face. He didn't have a lower jaw or a tongue. Marco asked him how it had happened, and of course Shrug just shrugged, then pointed to Stonewerth. Stonewerth later told Marco that the two of them had been in combat together, and the same explosion that had taken off her leg had cost Shrug the bottom half of his face. She didn't talk about the details, but Marco got the impression that one of them owed their life to the other for that incident.

On day twenty-four, Stonewerth had her own version of a breakdown, but rather than a bout of depression or a complex delusion, her particular form of dealing with stress consisted of actually acting like the commanding officer of their unit for the day. It was much like being back in boot camp, with incredibly long hikes, prolonged aiming training, and frequent push-ups for anyone who didn't fall in line. Interestingly, most of the Zeta Team seemed to appreciate the extra work. It made them feel like actual soldiers again, despite their exile.

On day twenty-five, Marco spent most of his day in the Complex with the three scientists. He went over old data regarding the ruins, simply reading as much as he could without trying to analyze any of it. About half-way through the day he relented to Doc as she wanted to do more "experiments," which she again declared inconclusive at the end. Hamlet thought this was pretty funny, and explained it when Doc was not around: apparently "inconclusive data" was Doc's way of saying she had actually orgasmed during the experience. As long as Marco kept giving her inconclusive data, she would keep asking him to return to her bed. Marco wasn't sure he would do it that often, though, as it still wasn't that much of a fun experience for someone to hook various electrodes to his body as foreplay and continually stop to measure his physiological response.

On day twenty-six he continued to read the ruins data. Hamlet was more than happy to share it with him, and even the rest of Marco's teammates in the Hall commented that maybe he would have been more suited to being one of the scientists than being one of the soldiers. Marco absolutely did not agree.

On day twenty-seven he stared at the ruins again. As he went to bed that night, Marco thought that maybe he now knew something about them that no one else had ever realized before.

And because of that, on day twenty-eight of Marco's time on 54174340, everything changed.

7

Marco woke up in Thorn's bed. She had a tendency to be a heavy sleeper, so he was able to leave the bed without rousing her. It wasn't that he had any problem with waking up next to her. There was no such thing as a "walk of shame" around here, and as long as everyone adhered to the "no means no" rule, there were no regrets for any intimate encounters, and no ribbing from anyone else regarding who you spent your time with and in what capacity. Marco simply slipped quietly out of her bed because, even after a month of the lax military standards of Zeta Team, he still kept a traditional military schedule. He couldn't sleep in if he tried, but unless it was one of those rare days when Stonewerth thought everyone else needed to be up to traditional standards, Marco didn't want to impose on anyone else.

By the time he finished his morning chemical shower (actual water was at a premium on Shithead, so it was never used for anything as decadent as cleaning) Stonewerth was also up and starting breakfast in the mess. By the lax rules of the Hall, Marco should have been the one to get breakfast going, as he had been the first one up, but after a while it had become evident that Marco would *always* be the first one up, and apparently his cooking, while not terrible, wasn't good enough that people wanted to eat it every day. Hamlet and Weirdlust soon joined them in the mess hall. While the scientists had their own kitchen facilities in the Complex, there were so few of them that they usually came over to the Hall instead. Just because they weren't military didn't mean the IPA soldiers didn't consider them part of Zeta Team, so they were always welcome.

"Morning," Weirdlust grumpily said to Marco as he sat down at a nearby table. Instead of joining him, Hamlet opted to sit in the seat opposite Marco.

"Why do we still even say 'good morning' around here?" Hamlet asked. "This isn't really morning by any of our typical standards. It's always dark out, and even according to the planetoid's rotation, this would be more like late afternoon."

"I say it because I feel like saying it," Weirdlust said. "And you're putting words into my mouth. I didn't say 'good morning.' I said 'morning.' There's a difference."

"What's gotten into you today?" Marco asked Weirdlust.

"Up late last night," Weirdlust said. "Doing experiments with Doc."

"Okay, were you doing experiments, or were you two doing 'experiments?'" Hamlet asked.

"Uh, the first kind, I think. The kind without the implied quotation marks. Doc is too much woman for me to do the other kind with her more than once every few weeks. Apparently Glare over there has gotten a bee in Doc's bonnet about looking back at the alien ruins data."

"Well, imagine that," Stonewerth said as she came over to their tables and gave them each a plate of something that was supposed to resemble bacon and eggs. Unfortunately, no matter how good a cook anyone on the team might be, it always ended up tasting more or less like tofu and other bland protein. "Someone here actually doing what they were sent here to do. Maybe that's the reason no one has ever made any discoveries about the ruins. No one is trying anymore."

"That, or no one is trying anymore because there's nothing to discover," Weirdlust said.

"I refuse to believe that," Hamlet responded. "Just because we can't figure the answers out doesn't mean they're not there."

Marco spoke slowly and precisely. He'd been thinking about this a lot, and he wanted everyone to take him seriously even if he wasn't part of the science team. "Actually, I think I may have figured something out."

Everyone in the mess hall stopped and stared at him. Even Tulip, who had just walked in and hadn't heard the beginning of the conversation.

"Are you talking about the ruins?" Tulip asked.

"Yes," Marco said.

"Bullshit," Weirdlust said. "People have been studying those things for nearly a century, and you think you've discovered something new with no scientific training and only twenty-eight days on the planet?"

"Now, hold on," Stonewerth said to Weirdlust. "Let's just listen to what the kid has to say."

Tulip left the mess hall. In the other room, Marco could hear her waking up the remaining three. Marco would have preferred that she didn't do that, but he knew by now that anything at all that broke up the monotony of life on Shithead was treated like it was a major event. Even if whatever Marco had to say was completely wrong, it would still likely be the most entertaining thing to happen all day.

"There's a pattern in the symbols that appear on the stones," Marco said.

"No there isn't," Hamlet said. "Even if it's too complex for any of us to pick up, aIdI would have picked it up by now."

"Well, I don't know about that," Weirdlust said. "aIdI is hardly the most up-to-date AI. She's been running our computers in the Complex for something like forty years, I think."

"Maybe it's because she's obsolete," Marco said, "or maybe it's because there was a simple human error in the way the symbols were recorded, an error that started the moment humans began to study them and that no one has caught in the entire century since."

"What kind of error?" Hamlet asked. Although he still sounded incredulous, he also was clearly excited at the idea of finally making some progress.

"Well, can someone grab me something to write with?" Marco asked.

"You mean physically write?" Weirdlust asked. "Just use a holo-pad."

"No, you see, that's where the error comes in. I need a piece of paper or cloth, and something to make marks on it."

This proved to be a harder task than anyone would have thought. The concepts of pen and paper had largely fallen by the wayside a long time ago. There was no need for them. If someone wanted to create some written record, they could just dictate it to a holo-pad or, if they were particularly old-fashioned, bring up the holo-pad's keyboard function. They had to actually go wake up Doc, who they had all witnessed using a form of pen and paper for her "experimental data" when they were intimate with her. By the time she had joined them, everyone else was awake and standing around Marco, most of them skeptical but all of them curious at the idea that the new guy had possibly cracked the code.

"Okay," Marco said. At random he picked Shrug and Spam out of the group. "You two. Each of you take a piece of paper and a pen. Go to opposite sides of the room so you can't see each other, and then write down the entire alphabet."

While they obviously thought this was weird, they did it without any question. Once they were done, they brought the paper back to Marco. Without letting anyone else see, Marco looked at them and smiled. After some thought he had Doc and Tulip do the same, then gathered up those papers as well.

"Okay, so?" Stonewerth asked. "What's all this supposed to prove?"

"Take a look," Marco said. He set the four pieces of paper down next to each other. Each person had done exactly as he said, yet all four of them had handed him something different. Hamlet had written down the twenty-six letters of the English-Arabic alphabet in a tight, practiced hand, even adding decorative seraphs to the letters to make it look just like the type he was used to in his beloved Shakespeare. Spam, however, had used his native L-and-C alphabet, which only had twenty-four letters. His handwriting was much sloppier, as well. Doc's was neat and tidy but only consisted of twenty-five because, according to her, "W isn't a real letter." Tulip's alphabet, like Spam's, was the regional variation of her own home world, giving it twenty-nine letters, and they were all done in a sweeping, feminine hand complete with hearts in place of dots in some of the letters.

"So what does this prove?" Thorn asked. "Because all of this looks pretty dumb and inconsequential to me."

"Take a look at these four pieces of paper and tell me how many letters are represented," Marco said. Once they started to count, though, he waved them off. "Actually never mind. Between these four pages there are thirty-one separate symbols. Except, if you were an alien race looking at these sheets of paper that we had left behind, how many different letters do you think you would see?"

"Um, thirty-one," Weirdlust said.

Shrug vehemently shook his head, then grabbed Doc's paper along with Spam's. He pointed at the M in both.

"Right," Marco said. "Spam's M is slanted, and not all the lines connect, and it's written in upper case. Doc's is in lower case, and so straight she could have used a straight edge to write it. We all recognize these two as the same letter because we're familiar with them. But if we weren't, we might think they are two separate letters."

"Oh God," Hamlet said softly. "How the hell did no one see this before now?"

"See what?" Stonewerth asked. "I still don't know what any of this is supposed to prove."

"All the symbols on the ruins are different fonts, or different handwritings, or maybe even different alphabets," Marco said. "When they were initially recorded, whoever did it just assumed that they were all done in the same style, because why wouldn't they be? And because we only use digital writing ourselves in most cases, everyone since has completely forgotten that it might be anything other than uniform. For the last hundred years, we've been acting like there are just over two hundred separate symbols on the ruins when they glow. We've been wrong. There's only eleven. They were just written in different dialects, or styles, or fonts or whatever. For over a century, we've been trying to read them the wrong way."

The mess hall went silent for several long moments, interrupted only by Weirdlust softly saying "Bullshit," although he didn't sound very convincing. Finally, Stonewerth stood up from where she'd been sitting and called out "Atennnnnn-shun!"

Marco immediately stood up at attention. It took the rest of the soldiers several seconds before they realized they were supposed to do the same.

"What's going on?" Hamlet asked.

"At this moment, I am invoking Protocol 1138," Stonewerth said. Thorn, Tulip, and Shrug all reacted like they'd just been smacked in the face with a fish.

"You can't be serious?" Thorn asked.

"I am serious," Stonewerth said.

"I still don't know what's happening," Hamlet said.

"Protocol 1138," Doc said. "Page 788 of the official Planetoid 54174340 Command Manual."

"There's an official command manual?" Weirdlust asked.

"Everyone is supposed to read it when they come to Shithead," Stonewerth said with a sneer. "But I've been lazy in enforcing it, as have a few of my predecessors, apparently. But we can't do that anymore." All of a sudden she was no longer the laid back commander Marco had gotten to know over the last twenty-seven days. This was someone who actually looked like she was about to prepare her troops for battle.

"Okay, that's all well and good, but what does Protocol 1138 actually do?" Weirdlust asked.

"There has been a new discovery regarding the alien artifacts," Stonewerth said.

"Oh come on, I wouldn't say that," Weirdlust said. "It's just a hypothesis. We haven't tested out Glare's theory yet. It could be completely wrong."

"How long will it take you to either prove him wrong or give some credence to the idea that he might be right?" Stonewerth asked.

"It could be days," Weirdlust said. "Maybe weeks."

"About two hours," Doc said.

"What? No!" Weirdlust said. "Don't go telling him that."

"I concur with Doc," Hamlet said. "Depending on how much help we can get from aIdI, anywhere from two hours until the end of the day at the latest."

"Get on it," Stonewerth said. "And bring Glare with you. He can double check any work you do."

Both Doc and Hamlet simply nodded at this. Weirdlust, on the other hand, looked positively offended that they were going to be overseen by an army grunt.

"What happens if it all checks out?" Thorn said. Although she spoke like her typical salty self, Marco couldn't help but notice the underlying thrill evident in her voice. All of the other IPA soldiers looked like they had it as well. Whether they had gotten lazy or not, all of them were ready for something different to finally happen.

"If it checks out, then I send a message to command, and Planetoid Shithead stops being the backwater where they send the screw-ups and has-beens. *We* stop being the screw-ups and has-beens. Soldiers, get your asses in gear and look sharp. If Glare is right, we're about to finally have company."

Marco would remember that sentence later, and it would occur to him that Stonewerth was correct, just not in the way any of them expected.

8

Weirdlust kept giving Marco the stink-eye for the entire time he helped the scientists out in the Complex. Finally, after an hour and a half of this angry silent treatment, Marco quietly asked Hamlet what his problem was.

"My guess," Hamlet said, "is that he's pissed at you for essentially just destroying his cushy job."

"What do you mean? I didn't destroy anything. I would have thought you three would be happy."

"Oh, I definitely am. I'm so ecstatic that I might just piss myself. This is exactly what I've wanted since I got here. I'm assuming Doc feels the same way, although no one can ever really tell with her. As long as she is 'sciencing', as she calls it, she's happy. This will probably actually make things easier around here, if this turns out to be something that can occupy her long-term. Fewer bizarre sexual encounters for all of us and, if I'm lucky, no more communicable diseases stored in the fridge next to the leftovers. But Weirdlust, he liked things the way they were. Since there was nothing much to do with the ruins, he had all the free time he wanted to work on his own projects. Now's he's actually expected to do the work he was brought here to do."

Personally, Marco couldn't understand why Weirdlust wouldn't be excited about this. Everything was going to change now. Not only was this going to suddenly be an important installation again, assuming all of Marco's theories checked out, but he was finally going to get his real last chance to show what he could do in the Interplanetary Army. Even beyond that, he was the one who had cracked a century-old mystery. He'd proven himself not to be the screw-up everyone believed him to be.

And most importantly of all, Horitz would be proud of him.

"aIdI?" Doc called out to the open lab around them. They had taken up residence for the time being in Hamlet's workspace, since he had already had most of the materials they needed to review queued up and ready to go. "You've been following everything we've been doing and saying, right?"

"Neck tie," a pleasant female voice chirped from various speakers throughout the room.

"I'm uploading what we've been working on to you now," Doc said. "Time to run it through all the other data you have and see if the symbols make more sense now."

"Neck tie," aIdI said again.

"Neck tie?" Marco asked Hamlet.

"Yeah, apparently some of our predecessors got bored and messed around with aIdI's vocabulary. Neck tie means 'affirmative,' and bacon means 'negative.' Be careful taking anything she says at face value. It might not mean what you think it means."

A holo-projector in the center of the room turned on to show a representation of aIdI. Unlike vIdI from the ship that had brought Marco here, aIdI was blockier and less defined. She looked vaguely like one of those small wooden models that artists sometimes used, except with vague facial expressions.

"Data processing alligator," aIdI said.

"She means she's done," Hamlet said to Marco.

"Wait, she can't be," Weirdlust said. "We only put in a couple weeks' worth of recorded symbols. There's no way she could take that and filter it through a hundred years' worth of data already."

"It was hard as hell," aIdI said.

"She means it was easy," Hamlet translated.

"Why doesn't anyone fix her vocabulary?" Marco asked.

"Honestly, because it kind of amuses us. And we're short of things to amuse us on this rock."

"But is she amused by it?" Marco asked.

"You know, I don't think any of us have ever thought to ask her," Hamlet said. "Hey, aIdI, do you want us to fix your vocabulary, or do you really not care?"

"Munchausen's by proxy," aIdI said.

"Yeah, that one I don't have the slightest clue on," Hamlet said.

Doc spoke up. "aIdI, if the data processing is complete, give us the results. Uh, I mean, show us the results. Don't try to say them. You'll probably give us all a headache."

"Neck tie," aIdI said. The image that the AI used as her avatar was replaced by several overlaying images of the symbols.

"Wow, you were really close," Hamlet said to Marco. "Fourteen separate symbols, written on the ruins in one hundred and eighty-nine different styles."

Marco went over to the display. "Is this an interactive holo-projector, or one of the old ones that you can't manipulate?"

"Just reach into the image and move things around, if you want," Doc said. "I do it all the time when I use it to compare the sizes of all your…"

"Doc, please," Hamlet said. "Now is not the time for that."

"aIdI, don't just project the symbols that have appeared, now," Marco said. "Project the stones that they're supposed to be on. Give us an image of them glowing and pulsing from the past."

The image turned into a miniature of the ruins. The symbols slowly glowed to life.

"Speed the video up," Marco said. "By, I don't know, maybe four times."

The glowing symbols appeared and vanished faster. The image also happened to catch the static discharge. Marco had been so preoccupied with the symbols that he had almost forgotten about the peculiarities he'd been seeing in the electricity, but now, seeing it all sped up, he saw that his first thoughts upon seeing the discharge had been right.

"Do you see it?" Marco asked everyone else.

"Um, no," Hamlet said.

"There's nothing to see, Glare," Weirdlust said. "You're just wasting our time."

"No, wait," Doc said. "I see it. aIdI, speed this up even more. One continuous recorded feed, no repeating at all."

aIdI did as she was told. With the video moving faster and the lightning erupting from the ruins every few seconds, it was now impossible for the others not to see what Marco had nearly noticed from the very beginning. The lightning flashed in one particular branching pattern, then another. Then, completely against everything they thought they knew about physics and electrical current, the first pattern repeated again. It wasn't just similar to the first pattern. It was exactly the same, right down to the tiniest twist in the electrical pulse. Electricity wasn't supposed to work like that. It could create a pattern that was very similar, but it should never be exactly the same.

Another pattern flashed, then a fourth. Then the second repeated, then the fourth again.

There was nothing random about the static discharges that erupted from the ruins. They were intentional. It wasn't just the symbols that had eluded them, but this as well.

"Son of a bitch," Hamlet whispered. "How is it possible that we've missed this for so long?"

"It's not exactly something we would ever typically think to look for, is it?" Weirdlust said. Even he seemed impressed now. "Lightning and electricity should never be that uniform. Ever."

"That's not even what I wanted to show you," Marco said. "aIdI, can you remove the discharge from the image? I just want to see the stones and the symbols now. Go back to the beginning of the video feed and start over, slightly slower."

As the image reset, Marco reached into it and manipulated one of the stones like he was lifting a light, physical object. He watched the way the symbols appeared and disappeared, then left the stone hanging in the air so he could grab another one. He compared the two, then pushed the second away and grabbed a third one.

"What are you doing?" Weirdlust asked. Hamlet shrugged at him. Doc, on the other hand, took up a position on the other side of the projector and started manipulating the pieces herself.

"I loved puzzles when I was a child," Doc said. "That's what this is."

"Do you all see?" Marco said over his shoulder to Weirdlust and Hamlet. "Once you recognize that most of the symbols are the same, just in different styles, then they no longer look so random when they appear and disappear. And, knowing that, if you were to put all the pieces together in the right places..."

"We should be able to reconstruct the ruins to their original shape and place," Hamlet said. "By figuring out the symbols, you essentially gave us the instruction manual to put it all back together."

"But put it all back together into what?" Weirdlust asked. He too joined Doc and Marco at the projector, with Hamlet close behind. For the next hour they worked in near silence, only talking when one thought they saw a mistake in the way one of their partners had placed a piece, or asking if they could have the piece someone else was examining because they thought it might fit well with one of the others. Finally Marco stepped away, satisfied, and the others did the same.

None of them spoke. The object in front of them pulsed with the symbols, but now they weren't random. The pulses ran in waves over the object, a complex pattern that they could only now see. But as much as Marco wanted to examine more of the nuances of the glowing pattern, he was more in awe of the object's final shape.

"Hey, are you guys thinking that this is the same thing I think it is?" Hamlet asked.

"Oh dear God," Weirdlust said. "If it is, then this is huge. If we put this all back together like this at the actual ruins, do you think it would work?"

Marco suspected that it would. Because the thing they had assembled was a complicated, ornate arch.

"aIdI, bring back the electrical currents," Doc said. "Make sure they're properly oriented with the current position of the stones."

The static began to flash in the image again. This time, instead of going up to disappear in the air, every bolt of lightning crossed into the center of the arch.

Marco spoke in a hushed tone. "It's a gateway."

"But a gateway to what?" Hamlet asked.

That, none of them could answer.

9

Everyone gathered back in the mess hall for dinner. Shrug took over the cooking duties, which everyone was happy about. For someone who couldn't actually taste anything and had to puree his food, he sure as hell knew how to cook. Once they all had a plate, Marco and the scientists told the rest of the Zeta Team exactly what they had seen. When they were finished, the entire population of Planetoid 54174340 was silent for a long time.

Stonewerth finally broke the silence by carefully standing up. "I know no one is going to like this, but per Protocol 1138, all research has to stop right now."

"Wait, what?" Hamlet asked. "You've got to be kidding!"

"No, I'm not kidding at all. Before anything can go any further, we need to bring in more people."

"So we make the find of a lifetime," Weirdlust said, "a discovery that will completely change the course of human history, and the first thing you do is impose bureaucratic red tape?"

To everyone's visible surprise, Thorn was the one who spoke up and answered. "We're dealing with a completely alien technology here. The nine of us alone wouldn't be able to handle it. I hate to be the one to break it to you all, but the reason we're here is because we suck."

Hamlet scoffed. "I don't suck."

"Sorry, Hamlet, but you do," Thorn said. "Or at least someone thinks you do. You may seem a lot more competent than Weirdlust…"

"Hey!" Weirdlust said.

"And you don't appear to have completely lost your marbles like Doc. Sorry, Doc. No offense."

"None taken," Doc said. "I lost my marbles when I was eleven. I think they might have rolled down a storm drain."

"But you still got sent here, Hamlet. In case no one figured it out yet, command gave up on unraveling the mysteries of Shithead long ago. You weren't *supposed* to make any new discoveries. You, Glare, Tulip, me, hell, even Stonewerth. They dumped us here for one reason: so they didn't have to deal with us anymore. So tell me honestly: do you really think any of us are prepared to do anything remotely useful in the event that the ruins get put back together and they actually do something?"

"We have no proof that they would," Weirdlust said. "They're just stones."

Spam spoke up. "Stones that glow and change with no apparent power source, and which emit electricity for no reason that we can explain with our current science. If Glare is right that this is some kind of gateway, then we can't make the assumption that it won't just start working by itself once it's put together."

Shrug waved to get their attention, then wrote something on one of the pieces of paper and showed it to them. *Even worse might be if it <u>doesn't</u> work right.*

"What do you mean?" Stonewerth asked.

"I think I get what he's saying," Spam said. "It's like if one of us tried to assemble a hyperdrive from scratch and then used it. None of us really knows how to do that, so one piece in the wrong place could result in us all getting blown up, or we try to use the hyperdrive and it sends us to the wrong place. Or creates a singularity. Or anything. We could try to put the ruins back together and instead vaporize the entire planetoid."

Thorn looked at her sister. "You're especially quiet. You don't have an opinion here?"

Tulip shrugged and smiled. "I just hope I get to meet aliens."

"It doesn't matter what anyone's opinion is," Stonewerth said. "We've had no reason to obey the rules for so long that we've forgotten that there are any. And the first rule is that this isn't a democracy. I'm the ranking officer here at the moment, so whatever I say goes. Second rule is that we call this in immediately. Third rule is that no one even goes near the ruins again until we're commanded otherwise."

"Do you think they will?" Tulip asked.

"Do I think who will what?" Stonewerth asked back.

"Do you think command will tell us to do something different?"

"I think..." Stonewerth slumped. For the first time during the conversation, she didn't look like she was in charge of anything at all. "I think that as soon as they bring in more capable scientists and soldiers, all of us are going to get shipped somewhere else."

"No!" Hamlet yelled. "That's bullshit!"

"We're the ones who made this discovery," Weirdlust said. "We should get to continue being a part of it."

"No, from where I'm standing, Glare is the one that made the discovery," Stonewerth said. "Trust me, after serving on this hell hole for so long, I'm just as upset as anyone at the possibility of being pushed aside just when things finally start to look meaningful. But when I make my report, I have to be honest. All of us were here for a very long time, and it amounted to nothing. Glare came in and changed it. He's going to get the credit, and if he chooses he will probably get to stay. All of the rest of us are going to go right back to being forgotten."

Everyone turned to stare at Marco. He'd listened to Stonewerth speak with a growing horror, knowing that all of a sudden he was going to be completely on the outs with the rest of the team. All he'd wanted to do was something meaningful, something worthy of his odd skills that would get him recognized. Well, now he was being recognized, and he was no longer sure he wanted it.

Thankfully, although they all appeared to be varying degrees of sad, the soldiers at least looked understanding. While Hamlet looked angry, he didn't necessarily look angry specifically at Marco. Doc didn't show much emotion at all. She just eyed Marco quizzically, and maybe even a little lustfully. Marco got the impression that his success here made him more interesting to her for her "experiments." Only Weirdlust looked completely pissed at Marco, which was kind of odd to Marco, considering the man had, only a few hours ago, not wanted anything to do with the ruins at all.

"Okay then," Stonewerth said. "That should settle everything. Eat up and then head on back to your places. Those of you in the Complex, you are expressly forbidden from doing any further work regarding the ruins. Entertain yourselves with something else. Knowing you guys, it shouldn't be that hard. Those of you in the Hall, you better take advantage of tonight, because starting tomorrow you're all going to be expected to follow strict IPA procedures and routines. We're going to have company coming, after all. We're going to need to look like we haven't been sitting on our asses and making up nonsensical sports the whole time."

"But that *is* what we've been doing," Tulip said.

Stonewerth sighed. "Yes, I know that. But let's not look like it."

Stonewerth started to storm out of the mess hall, but she stopped at the entrance and turned back. "Private Marco Cruz, I'm going to need you to come with me to do this report." She sounded weary, as if she was already tired of all the changes that were about to descend on them. Marco left the remainder of his dinner on the plate and followed her, stopping only long enough to look back and gauge the emotions of everyone else. His keen perception for details failed him now, though, as everyone but Weirdlust hid their emotions well.

The two of them went all the way back to a small room at the rear of the Hall that Marco had never been in before. In fact, it looked like no one had been in here for quite some time, given the large pile of junk that had been heaped around the door. Most of it looked like outdated communications equipment, the kind that had been replaced by the much faster and far more efficient hyper-link technology the Interplanetary Army used now. Marco helped Stonewerth move just enough of the rusting equipment that they were able to get the door open.

"Why is this old equipment even still here?" Marco asked. "At any other base it would have been melted down and repurposed by now."

"You just answered your own question," Stonewerth said. "We're not any other base. It's too inefficient to send a ship all the way out here to collect our garbage, and no one higher in command wants to spend the money for us to have more than the most basic incinerators and recyclers. We don't have anything to take care of the larger equipment. If you think this is bad, you should see some of the storage areas in the Complex. There's junk in there going all the way back to the original founding of the base. I couldn't even begin to tell you what some of that stuff is supposed to be used for."

They went through the door to a room that was barely able to accommodate the two of them together along with all the equipment inside. This would be how 54174340 kept track of what was going on in the outside universe, but it didn't look like any of it had been used in quite some time.

Stonewerth answered the question before Marco could even ask it. "This isn't the only equipment we have. I have a smaller unit that I can use for basics. That's how we knew that they were sending a new guy, and it's how we told them we had a space open. It's also how we know the entire rest of the universe hasn't gone and gotten itself vaporized while we were busy smashing each other up with clubs in Sportsball. But it's not as secure as the equipment in here. Using this, we'll be able to send a signal directly to a small number of very important people. It's faster than the hand unit, too. It can send a message across the light years almost as fast as we could send a ship."

They had to squeeze together for both of them to get in front of the holo-screen. It might have been awkward if they were less familiar with each other, but by this point they'd seen each other naked, so there wasn't a lot left to be embarrassed about. That memory, though, suddenly made Marco squirm. Not because he was ashamed that he'd had sex with Stonewerth and other members of Zeta Team, but because he knew all of that was more or less over. It was like they'd all been on an extended vacation up until now. It might have been an incredibly boring vacation, but it had still been time off from any real expectations.

"How much does command know about what goes on here on Shithead?" Marco asked.

Stonewerth snorted. "If you're worried that you're going to get in trouble for carnally knowing your superior officer, don't worry about it. The higher-ups know all about that stuff, and they've made it known in the past that they don't care. As long as they don't have to deal with us, that's all that usually matters to them. Or at least that's the way it used to be. I doubt any of us will be punished for how lax we've been in the past, but the free ride is over as soon as we send this message."

Stonewerth flipped a few switches on the equipment. The holo-screen came to life and informed them that it was establishing a secure hyper-space beam. Not that Marco knew exactly how that worked, but he knew it would take roughly ten minutes before it was ready for them to transmit any signal.

"Major, do you mind if I ask why you got stuck here with us?" Marco asked.

"I told you, don't call me major," Stonewerth said.

"It's Stone or Stonewerth up until the moment someone shows up and forces us to start using ranks again."

"You used my rank earlier."

"I guess I did, didn't I? I suppose I'm already subconsciously getting ready for our big change."

"You didn't answer my question," Marco said.

"Well, it's a pretty straightforward answer. They stuck me here because I spit on someone with a higher rank."

"Wait, really?"

Stonewerth gave a small smile as she sat down in a creaky chair. There was only the one seat, so Marco continued to stand at attention. Even after a month, that habit still hadn't died in him.

"Yep. I guess that I'm supposed to tell the people under me that it wasn't one of my finer moments, but I would be lying. The memory still makes me chuckle myself to sleep at night."

"Why?"

Stonewerth's smile disappeared. "You've seen my leg, of course."

"Of course."

"And you've also seen the ruins of Shrug's face. I don't know how many rumors you've picked up, but the two of us got those injuries at the same time. It happened during an offensive against the Maxlin Uprising on Cernunnos."

"I remember that. I was a kid at the time. I guess that would make the two of you older than you look."

"Yeah, strangely enough, the drugs Shrug and I have to take to keep our cybernetics compatible with our immune systems, they also seem to slow cell death in the skin. Our insides are old, but our outsides look about twenty years younger. But that's not the point. The point is, I saved a bunch of people, and then Shrug saved me, but not before nearly getting ganked by a thermite grenade. I found out afterward that the man in charge, who got a commendation for the offensive, by the way, actually sat on some vital information that could have gotten us out of there before we got screwed. So when he came to visit me in the hospital and congratulate me on a job well done, and to hand me my medals and yadda yadda yadda, I spit on him. On live holo-vision."

Marco sucked in a breath. "Ow. Okay. Now I get it."

"So there I was, considered a hero, so they couldn't punish me as much as they wanted, but they had to do something. So here I am. Shrug just followed because he felt obligated to me."

"So you weren't like some of the others around here," Marco said. "You really believed in your place among the IPA?"

"I did up until I found out about what really happened on Cernunnos. After that, I was perfectly fine slacking here. I figured I earned it."

The holo-image in front of them flickered. Stonewerth frowned and smacked the side of the main processor. "That would just be great, wouldn't it? The comm units going out right when we actually need them for a real reason."

The display went from showing that the hyper-beam uplink was fifty-six percent complete to one percent.

"What the hell?" Stonewerth asked.

"Have you had this kind of problem with it before?" Marco asked.

"No, but it's not like we ever really had a need to use it. The occasional short test run worked just fine."

The progress bar crawled up to four percent, then vanished with the message *Hyper-Beam Uplink Failed*.

"Son of a bitch," Stonewerth said. "We're going to have to get one of the eggheads in here to find out what's wrong with it."

"I don't think the equipment is the problem," Marco said quietly. "Listen."

Stonewerth turned the comm equipment down so they could listen to the subtle buzz coming from outside. After a few seconds Stonewerth asked, "What even is that?"

"When I was younger, I lived with my mom near some power lines," Marco said. "There was a constant hum in the background that you could never not hear. It sounded almost exactly like this."

"Electricity," Stonewerth said.

The two of them looked at each other, immediately

understanding what was going on. Stonewerth ran out of the room with Marco close behind. Tulip and Thorn were in the mess hall cleaning the dishes, although both of them had been distracted by the sound.

"What's going on?" Tulip asked.

"Where's everyone else?" Stonewerth asked.

"Uh, Spam and Shrug were talking about getting in one last game of Sportsball, or at least Spam was," Thorn said.

"What about the other three?" Stonewerth asked.

Thorn shrugged. "As far as I know they went back to the Complex."

"All of them?" Marco asked.

"Well, yeah, but now that I think of it, Weirdlust seemed to be in more of a hurry than the other two."

"Shit!" Stonewerth said. "Everyone, grab your weapons!"

"What?" Tulip asked. "Who are we supposed to fight?"

"If we're lucky, just Weirdlust," Stonewerth said as she herself ran for the weapons rack. "If we're not lucky, then maybe a whole lot more."

10

Stonewerth was the first out the front door of the Hall, which meant that she was the one who ran head-first into Doc as she tried to come in. The two of them sprawled in a mess of arms and legs in the doorway, effectively blocking anyone else from getting out.

"Smooth," Thorn said. "If aliens really are coming, I'm sure they're looking at us right now and really quaking in their boots."

"Come on, you don't really think we're about to be invaded or something, do you?" Spam asked her.

"We can't make any assumptions," Stonewerth said as she extricated herself from Doc.

"You guys have to get out there!" Doc yelled at them.

"In case you haven't noticed, we're trying," Thorn said.

"I'm going to go out the other door!" Tulip said as she ran to the other side of the Hall.

"Tulip, stop!" Thorn called after her. "By the time you get out the door and get around to the front again, we'll be… ah, forget about it. She's gone."

Stonewerth and Doc both got to their feet. "Doc, what the hell is happening?" Stonewerth asked.

"Weirdlust and Hamlet went over to the ruins," she said. "And they took the spinning tower thingies with them."

"The who what now?" Spam asked.

"Shouldn't we suit up with our tactical armor?" Marco asked.

"Okay, everyone just shut up!" Stonewerth said. "Jesus, this is what we get for going so lax."

"This can't be that big of a deal, can it?" Spam asked. "I mean, those stones are huge anyway. Even if putting the ruins back in place somehow activated them, the two of them alone couldn't move anything by themselves, right?"

The humming in the air increased, and with it the entire Hall started to vibrate.

"Just get out to the ruins and stop whatever the hell those two idiots are doing!" Stonewerth yelled.

Despite Thorn's admonition to her sister, Tulip was the first one of them to the ruins. She was also sprawled flat on the ground when they found her. Beyond, Weirdlust and Hamlet were next to several of the stones. Weirdlust was actively trying to push one so it connected with another, and despite their size and weight, he was somehow moving them rather easily. Hamlet stood off to the side, looking back at Tulip with a distinct look of worry.

"Forget about her!" Weirdlust said. "Just help me before they find a way to stop us!"

As the others rushed forward, Marco pulled himself up short as he saw the objects Doc had mentioned. They weren't towers so much as high-tech looking poles, or at least what high-tech might have looked like decades earlier. The end of each one, six in all, had been shoved into the rocky dirt surrounding the ruins to form a very loose circle. Something near the top of each one that looked like a turbine spun in a counter-clockwise direction. Although Marco had never seen this specific design before, he intuited almost immediately their purpose.

"No! Stop!" he yelled at Stonewerth and the others. They had all continued barreling ahead, their IPA-issue rifles out ahead of them, as they ran right for Weirdlust. Only Doc had stopped along with Marco, presumably because she knew just as well as Marco what the six poles were there for.

Stonewerth heard Marco in time and tried to pull up short. Thorn also skidded to a halt next to her sister to make sure she was okay. Spam and Shrug, however, kept running, which meant they went face first into the invisible barrier in front of them. Apparently it was only invisible when nothing touched it, because the places where they hit flashed a deep purple as they bounced off and fell flat on the ground next to Tulip.

"God damn it!" Stonewerth screamed, then turned and looked at Doc. "What the hell is this thing?"

"Portable one way forcefield generators," Doc said.

"And why the hell do you guys just have something like this lying around for you to use during a mutiny?" Thorn asked as she helped her sister to her feet. Tulip was dazed and had a small trickle of blood running from her nose, but she appeared to otherwise be okay.

"I'm betting these were in that pile of junk in the Complex

you were talking about," Marco said to Stonewerth.

"We found them about a year ago," Doc said. "We played around with them for a little bit before we got bored with them and forgot them. I think they were part of the original security measures they had ready when a base was first established here, but after it became apparent that nothing was going to be discovered, they went back into storage."

"You idiots!" Stonewerth screamed at the pair within the circular force field. "I order you to stop whatever the hell it is you're doing!"

Hamlet came up to the edge of the force field. Weirdlust acted like he didn't even know anyone was there, and kept working at the stones. To Marco, it looked almost like he was executing some feats of superhuman strength to pick up the blocks and move them around.

"Look, you guys need to calm down," Hamlet said. "Nothing is going to happen. This whole thing is getting blown out of proportion."

"Hamlet, don't you feel the way everything is shaking?" Spam asked as Shrug helped him up.

"That's just from the force field generators," Hamlet said, although he didn't sound too sure about that. "All we're going to do is move a few of the stones around to see if they react. It's a harmless experiment, and given that we're the ones who've been stuck here with the ruins this whole time, we think we have the right to do it. We're not going to let someone else come in and take all the glory when we're the ones that put in the hours here."

Marco grabbed Doc by the shoulders. "How do we turn off the generators?"

"Easy," Doc said. "Just flip any one of the switches on the towers. All six of them have to be on for them to form the force field."

"Great! So where are the switches?"

"On the inside of the field."

"Doc, you're really not helping."

"Hamlet, you need to stop right now," Stonewerth said. "Whatever Weirdlust is doing with the stones, it's actually enough to cause interference on the hyper-beam array. Do you know what kind of energy something has to be giving off to affect a hyper-beam?"

"But he's not even doing anything," Hamlet said as he turned to look at Weirdlust. "He's just trying to push some of the..." He stopped and stared at his companion. "Holy crap. How is he lifting those?"

"I don't think he is," Marco said. "I think he just thinks he is."

Hamlet ran up to Weirdlust and grabbed him by the arm. Weirdlust stopped and tried to shrug Hamlet off. While he stopped, however, the stone kept moving through the air without him. Both Hamlet and Weirdlust looked at the levitating stone with a combination of shock and growing dread.

"Doc, really, we have to turn the force field off," Marco said to her. "There has to be a way, right?"

"No. You can't even try to go over it. It creates a bubble around the six towers. If they were in mode one, we'd be able to get in, but they're in mode two."

"What does that mean?" Thorn said to her. She had to raise her voice, as the low hum was quickly becoming a rumble, and air rushed out from the direction of the ruins as though the stones themselves were preparing to release a cyclone.

"The force field only works one way at a time," Doc said. "You can go through it from one side, but not the other. Based on some of the old notes I found in the archives, they seem to have been designed to go up around the ruins and provide the field to keep anything alien inside, while soldiers on the outside could still shoot in at any threat. But Hamlet and Weirdlust reversed the direction of the field. They can get out from inside, but no one can get in."

"What about power?" Spam asked her. "Isn't there some kind of, I don't know, battery we can pull on them?"

"They wouldn't be very good at generating a force field if they were that easy to beat, now would they?" Doc said. She had to practically scream now to be heard over the wind and buzzing. "We didn't find exactly what powered them when we were playing with them, but there's got to be something about that in the notes."

Inside the field, both Weirdlust and Hamlet had begun to back away from the ruins as several of the stones lifted up of their own accord and floated through the air. It was obvious that the stones were attempting to form the shape Marco and the scientists had created in the holo-display, and every time one of the stones fit into place, the wind and noise increased. Electricity began to shoot out of several of the stones, converging in the center of the arch they were forming.

"How did this even start?" Spam asked. "The ruins have been sitting dormant for a hundred years. Hell, probably a hell of a lot longer than that even before we found them. Why are they doing this now?"

Hamlet ran up to join them. "Weirdlust just pushed a few in the right direction. With each push they got easier to move," he said, then stopped when he saw everyone staring at him incredulously. "What?"

"You're on this side of the force field now," Thorn said to him.

"Yeah? That's how it works. I can cross over from that side."

"But you can't get back," Marco said.

"Do you not see what's going on in there?" Hamlet asked. "I don't want to go back."

"Hamlet, for someone who's supposedly so smart, you have to be one of the dumbest people I've ever met!" Stonewerth said. "If you're on this side and you can't go back in, *then you can't turn the force field off!*"

Under any other situation, the play of emotions across Hamlet's face would have been comical. In the space of only two seconds he went from angry to confused and uncomprehending, followed soon after by a dawning horror that slowly crept over him, starting with his eyes, then his mouth, and finally taking over his entire face.

"Oh God," Hamlet whispered. Or at least that's what Marco thought he whispered. The background noise was too great for Marco to do more than read his lips. Hamlet spun around and screamed at Weirdlust within the force field. "Weirdlust, don't run out! Turn the field off first!"

Weirdlust had looked for a second like he was about to repeat Hamlet's mistake, but at Hamlet's words he pulled up short, nodded, and then ran in the direction of the nearest pole. Behind him, the stones finished levitating in place. Up until now there had been clear gaps between the various pieces, but as the last stone slipped into place there was a blinding flash that caused everyone to look away. When Marco looked back, he saw one continuous piece of stone. If he were seeing it now for the first time, he wouldn't have believed that it was previously broken into smaller chunks. The flash had blinded Weirdlust as well, causing him to trip just short of one of the poles. As he struggled to stand back up, the archway pulsed with color. The glowing symbols all returned at once, showing brighter than they ever had before. Then they all vanished.

Marco knew exactly what would happen next. He just wasn't prepared for the sheer violence of it.

Just as always, seconds after the symbols disappeared, the archway released a discharge of static electricity. This time, however, with all the pieces working in tandem as one, the lighting within the gateway was enough to cause an explosive concussion wave that knocked everyone flying several feet back in the air. Marco was on the ground and dazed from the impact for several seconds before he realized that all sound had stopped except for a ringing in his ears. When he sat up he saw Tulip on the ground next to him, obviously trying to speak to him despite Marco's inability to hear her. She stopped soon after, though, when she realized she couldn't even hear herself.

Even as the ringing subsided and Marco's hearing returned, the world around them remained mostly silent. Stonewerth was already up on her feet, although she did nothing more than stare at the arch in grim fascination. The humming and electrical buzz in the air had mostly stopped. Marco thought it might still be there in a greatly diminished form, or else the tingling he still felt was an after effect of the electrical explosion. Everyone else stood up soon after, each of them turning to look in silence at the alien gateway.

Marco had hoped for a moment that the blast would have dislodged the poles keeping up the force-field, but something in their construction must have resisted the electrical pulse. The archway itself was roughly two stories tall and four meters across. Now that it was in one piece, the stone appeared to shine in a pearlescent fashion, as though the entire thing had been carved from a single impossibly large opal. It didn't glow though, and there was no true sign that it would again in the future.

Except, for all the gateway's majesty, that wasn't the object inside the circular force field that drew everyone's attention. Instead they all stared at the large prism shape that had been ejected from the gateway during the blast. It was eight sided and probably just under two meters long from tip to tip. It appeared to be made of stone just like the individual pieces had earlier, and also like them, multi-colored symbols pulsed along the sides, appearing first on one face, then another, before they disappeared from the first face and the process started again. The whole prism was partially imbedded in the ground at an angle like an unusually wide javelin that had been thrown from a distance.

And the point of the javelin had gone right through Weirdlust.

It had pierced him from behind and pinned him to the ground like an enormous pin through a butterfly on display. Blood had splattered the ground all around him. It was impossible to tell if Weirdlust had been alive for any of the precious seconds it had taken the team to regain their senses, but he was definitely dead now.

He had never reached the off switch for the force field. Anything else that might come through the gateway could come out at them, but they couldn't get in.

11

"The hyper-beam uplink is completely screwed."

Stonewerth sat down at the end of her bed and ran a hand through her hair. For the last forty-five minutes she had been in the comm room trying to get the equipment to work properly. During that time, the seven other remaining citizens of Planetoid Shithead had been sitting, standing, or pacing at various places throughout the main room of the Hall. None of them had spoken during that entire time. Even Doc, who was usually good for some kind of inane or incoherent patter, wouldn't speak. No one here could have been said to be exactly close to Weirdlust, but he had been one of them. Now, not only was he dead, but they couldn't do anything about his body. It was just stuck there beyond the force field while the enigmatic object from the gateway continued to pulse with its symbols. No one had wanted to stay out there, but at the same time no one had wanted to do anything to take their mind off what had happened. They had just stayed there in the Hall, hoping that Stonewerth would come out with the good news that backup was on its way to relieve them of being the only ones who could puzzle this all out.

And now, apparently, even that wasn't going to happen. "What the hell do you mean that it's screwed?" Thorn asked. "That stuff is supposed to be the most sophisticated equipment we've got on the whole planetoid."

"It just keeps failing to establish the link after about fifteen minutes of trying," Stonewerth said. "I was trying to scour through the instruction manual to find out what might have happened. Apparently that's a sign that the hyper-beam is experiencing interference at a key point in the uplink, or something like that."

"Either me or Doc could try looking at it, see if we might be able to do something you can't," Hamlet said softly. Out of everyone, he had been the one that looked the closest to tears this entire time. Although he'd been as silent as everyone else, Marco thought maybe he blamed himself for what had happened. And judging from the way several of the soldiers kept their distance, the majority of the people here agreed with him.

"Do either of you have any expertise in that sort of thing?" Stonewerth asked.

"Not really. My specialty is materials and chemistry. Doc's best at biology. Weirdlust was the one we usually turned to for tech or engineering reasons."

"We still might be able to do something, though," Doc said. "At the very least, we've got to know more about it than anyone else."

Stonewerth pointed with her thumb over her shoulder, indicating the comm room. "Be my guest. You certainly can't do any worse than me."

"And what if they can't do anything?" Tulip asked as the two remaining scientists went to see what they could do. "Don't we have another way to communicate with command?"

"I've got my hand unit," Stonewerth said, "but I've been trying that the entire time, too. It works on a different frequency than the main unit, but it still uses the same technology. If the reason the main unit isn't working is because of the arch or gateway or whatever it is, then the hand unit has to be experiencing the same interference."

"So we can't call anyone at all?" Spam asked. "We're completely cut off."

"It looks like it," Stonewerth said.

"What about if someone tries to call us instead of us calling them?" Marco asked. "Won't they realize something is wrong then?"

"Yes, they probably will. And they would send an emergency ship to come check on us," Stonewerth answered. "There's just one problem with that: they only ever bother to ping us to make sure we're all alive once every two Earth-standard weeks. And guess when the last time was that they did a check in?"

"Yesterday?" Thorn asked.

"Day before, actually," Stonewerth said. "So we have a minimum of twelve days before anyone realizes something's wrong."

"That doesn't seem so bad," Tulip said. "We survive without their help all the time. It's not like we don't have the supplies to last us that long."

"It took my ship two weeks to get here," Marco said. "If they can speed the process up, maybe they could get a ship here in ten days. So twenty-two days in all. We can do that."

Thorn snorted. "Sure. We could do that just fine, unless something were to happen like, oh, I don't know, the gateway suddenly erupting and showering more of those prism things all over both the Hall and the Complex."

"Thorn's right," Stonewerth said. "We need to assume that whatever the hell happened here today is going to happen again. So I guess that means that the first thing we do, before we even try anything else at all, is find out what the hell exactly *did* happen. Anyone have any ideas? And if anyone tries to give some kind of snarky answer, I swear to God I'm going to take my rifle and butt-stroke you upside the head with it. We've completely run out of time to goof off."

No one spoke for a long time. Thorn was finally the one who broke the silence. "We did all see the same thing, right? The arch put itself together?"

"It sure looked like that to me," Spam said. "Hamlet said the stones got easier to move the closer they were to being where they were supposed to be."

"So how does that happen?" Stonewerth asked.

"It has to be some kind of technology we've never seen before," Marco said.

"What technology?" Thorn asked. "They were fricking *rocks*. They've been studied for years. You would think if there was some kind of circuit boards or software or something like that inside, the sciencey types would have found it a long time ago."

"They glowed and changed with the symbols," Tulip said. "They were never just stones."

"It's some level of technology humans haven't reached yet," Marco said. "If we could never detect what caused the glowing symbols, we sure weren't going to detect some aspect of the tech that would allow it to put itself together."

"But again," Stonewerth said, "if they could do that, why didn't they before?"

"Weirdlust moved a few," Tulip said.

"So what? Don't try to tell me none of our predecessors never tried to move them."

"It has to have been the specific way they were moved," Marco said.

Thorn shook her head. "Yeah. It's almost like someone who's too observant for his own damned good came along and figured out the right pattern. Any idea who that might have been, Glare?"

"Alright, you stop that shit right there," Stonewerth said to her in a tone that clearly said she wasn't going to allow any talking back. "There's not going to be any blaming of anyone else. That includes blaming Glare for figuring it all out, Hamlet for his lapse of judgment, and definitely not Weirdlust. The guy might have had the personality of a doorknob sometimes, but he's dead and gone, and we're not going to rip on someone who can't defend himself. Do I make myself completely clear?"

Thorn looked stunned, but she sat up straighter and nodded. "Crystal clear, major."

Not *Stone* or *Stonewerth*, Marco noticed, but *major*. Somehow, out of all the crazy things that had happened so far, that felt like the clearest sign that something significant had changed. As he looked around at the others, he got the feeling that they felt it too.

Yesterday they had been the screw-ups, losers, and has-beens of the Interplanetary Army. Today, from this moment on, those titles didn't mean anything anymore. The only title that mattered now was *soldier*.

"Let's get back on track," Stonewerth said. "Let's say that the reason the stones moved by themselves was that they had some kind of programming that told them to do so when they were put into specific positions. But why? We keep referring to this thing as a gateway, but is that really the case? What's the purpose of any of it?"

"I suppose I kind of thought that once it was together we were going to get some kind of alien invasion," Thorn said. "I have to say that having it shoot out another damned rock wasn't really a possibility I saw."

"That's because you always assume the worst," Tulip said. "'Ooh, there's ruins left behind by ancient aliens, so it must have something to do with destroying us.' How do we know the aliens didn't use it as a puppy generator or something?"

"Puppies?" Spam asked. "What, you think that stone thing that came through the arch and crushed Weirdlust is their version of a pet?"

Tulip shrugged. "Who knows? They're aliens."

"Maybe the prism thing is more technology we don't understand yet," Marco said. "We don't know the real purpose of the arch, but we know it can do a whole lot more than just sit there. We should make the same assumption with the prism."

"We need to have the scientists study it more," Stonewerth said. "And Marco, since you're the one who set this in motion, you're probably the one who can help them continue to figure it out. The rest of us have to set up some kind of defensive perimeter near the prism."

Marco nodded, although he wasn't especially happy about this. He was here to be a soldier. He wanted to be with the rest guarding the prism and the arch. It was slowly growing apparent, though, that the proper place for his unique talents might not be in the IPA after all. He might have wanted to follow in Horitz's footsteps, but his way of seeing patterns had been detrimental in that line of work. Maybe his place all along had never really been in the Hall. He was one of the scientists, whether he liked it or not.

"A defensive perimeter?" Thorn asked. "Really? What exactly are you expecting that prism to do?"

"I don't know. Explode? Fire lasers? Maybe Tulip is the one who's right and it's going to start spitting out puppies and kittens. Until we know for sure, we're going to work with the assumption that it's some kind of weapon. I want two people out there watching it at all times, starting now. Tulip, Shrug, you've got first watch. Try to maintain a safe distance from it, but be close enough to shoot anything that might try to get out of that force field. We'll start with two hour shifts. Now hop to it, you two."

Tulip and Shrug stood and went to put on their battle armor. Once they were completely suited up they left, and soon after that, Hamlet and Doc came back out of the communications room.

"There's nothing wrong with the equipment itself as far as I can tell," Doc said. "Something's jamming the signal."

"And since there's not supposed to be anything that can jam a hyper-beam uplink," Hamlet said, "we're going to have to assume that the arch is the one doing it."

"Great," Stonewerth said. "So we've got maybe twenty-four days or so before anyone comes searching for us. There's got to be some other way around that."

"Actually, I think I have an idea," Doc said. "You see, if we take…"

Tulip came bursting back in through the door before she could finish. "Major, I think we might have a problem."

12

Here they all were again, standing just outside the force field and trying to make sense of what they saw beyond. Had they not all been tuned into the potential dangers of any changes in the situation at all, Tulip and Shrug might have taken one look at the prism and assumed nothing of note had changed. It was still in exactly the same position as it had been before, and Weirdlust's remains were still pinned under it. There were two major differences to the scene from when they had last all looked at it, though.

The first was that the prism was no longer glowing. The symbols had completely disappeared, just like they always had on the stones after a discharge. But rather than just going on to look like a normal stone, the prism now looked more porous, less like a solid piece of rock than like a giant, desiccated sponge.

The second difference was Weirdlust. His body hadn't been moved, but it was now shriveled, almost mummified, like something had sucked all the moisture out of it.

"Did the prism do that to him?" Spam asked.

"It must have," Hamlet said. "Unless you know of some other reason that might have happened in less than an hour. Planetoid Shithead may be dry and arid, but not *that* dry."

Shrug tapped Tulip on the shoulder, then pointed at the prism. He made a gesture with his hands like he was holding something that was crumbling apart.

"Yeah, if you're trying to say what I think you are, then I think you're right," Tulip said. "It's disintegrating. The stone looks like it's in even worse shape than it did a few minutes ago when we first found it like this."

"If that's true, its breakdown probably started just recently," Doc said. "Otherwise, at that rate, if it had begun breaking down after it was ejected from the arch, it would be nothing but powder by now."

"So what changed?" Stonewerth asked.

As if in response, Marco felt a hum in the air again. The

pearlescence of the arch faded, again being replaced by the glowing symbols.

"That, maybe?" Thorn said. "It looks like it's getting back in gear to do that electrical flash thing again."

"Yeah, and when it does, I'd bet good money that another one of these prism things is going to come out," Stonewerth said. She turned to face everyone. "We go back to what we were originally planning. Marco and Hamlet, get your butts into the Complex and start trying to work this problem. Tulip and Shrug, same orders as before. Thorn, Spam, you two try to rest. I want you ready and able once it's time for your watch. Doc, come with me back to the comm room. You sounded like you had an idea."

Everyone hastily went about their orders with the exception of Marco, who took just enough time to go back to the Hall to grab his battle gear and weapons. While he knew he wasn't going to need it while studying the ruins with Hamlet, he still wanted to have everything at hand in the event that an alarm went out and he would be expected to join the others again. Once he was in the Complex with Hamlet, the scientist pointed at the armored breast plate and shoulder pads Marco carried. His rifle and side arm were in the other hand, which meant he had no choice but to wear his helmet loosely on his head.

"Aren't you supposed to actually wear that for it to be effective, or do you just really want to protect your hand?"

"I want it all ready, but I don't want it to get in the way while we're working."

"You're a person stuck between two worlds, Glare. Eventually you're going to have to pick one and stick with it."

"The world I want to be a part of doesn't want me, though," Marco said. "Otherwise I wouldn't be here."

"You're right, you wouldn't. You also wouldn't be on the one planetoid in the whole galaxy where your ability to see things others don't was desperately needed."

They set themselves up in Hamlet's lab. His workspace was cleaner than Doc's or Weirdlust's, but it was still strewn with various odds and ends in peculiar places. Apparently Planetoid Shithead could mess with even the most fastidious scientist and slowly transform him into a slob.

"Alright then, first question," Hamlet said. "Where do we even start with this?"

"Let's bring aIdI online in here," Marco said. "Whatever aspect of this we start working on, we're probably going to need her help."

"You heard him, aIdI," Hamlet called out to the room. "Get your digital butt out here."

A holo-projector in the floor surged to life to show aIdI's blocky avatar. "Wolverines!" aIdI called out. In as much as was possible for an AI, she sounded alarmed.

"What does that mean?" Marco asked Hamlet. Hamlet frowned and shook his head.

"I've never heard her say that before, so I couldn't tell you."

"Wolverine sandwich!" aIdI said. With every word, she seemed more and more agitated. Marco didn't even know that AIs *could* be agitated. "Sandwich full of wolverines! Eat the sandwich!"

"Damn it, now I really wish we'd gotten our asses in gear and fixed her vocabulary earlier," Hamlet said.

"Can you do it now?" Marco asked.

"Maybe? I can try. But again, Weirdlust is the one we would have wanted working on that. My knowledge of that kind of thing is more rudimentary."

"Try," Marco said. While Hamlet left the room to go access aIdI's central core, which was apparently deep in one of the storage rooms, Marco went up to the holo-image and did his best to sooth her, if she even could be soothed. "aIdI, we'll figure out what you're trying to tell us. But until then we're going to need your help figuring out what's happening with the arch."

A light bulb appeared over aIdI's head. People hadn't even bothered to use old-style light bulbs in a very long time, but apparently when it came to representations of AIs, they still represented having ideas.

"Wolverine sandwich," she said again, although now it was with an approximation of determination rather than agitation. "Eat it now." Her avatar disappeared and was replaced with a video feed from outside the Complex, pointed at the ruins. The feed didn't seem to be live, though. Although the video was from some distance, Marco could see the prism and Weirdlust's body, both of them as they had been earlier.

"Are you trying to show me something specific?" Marco asked. "If you are, enhance the place you're trying to show me."

The feed zoomed in on the prism and fixed the resolution so he could clearly see as Weirdlust's body shriveled beneath the prism. The symbols on it strobed faster, until suddenly they went out.

Given what Marco had seen before, he would have expected the prism to release yet another static discharge.

It released something, alright, but it wasn't electricity.

At first there was a blinding flash, but then it looked like something absorbed all the light, pulling it all in to cause a single dark spot on the image of the prism. The spot grew, spreading out over the prism like an oil slick. It covered the entire surface of the object, then somehow managed to get darker even than before. The absence of light and color somehow managed to hurt Marco's eyes more than the flash had, so he couldn't help but look away for a few seconds. When he looked back, he got a fleeting glimpse of something zipping out of view, something too dark and fast for him to make any sense of it, even with his quick knack for picking up details. The prism started to have the porous appearance they'd just seen.

"aIdI, how long ago was this video feed taken?" Marco asked.

"Thirty broccoli ago."

Assuming "broccoli" meant minutes, that would mean that this had happened about five to ten minutes before Tulip and Shrug had discovered the change in the prism. Whatever had come out of it, it could be anywhere now.

And yet Marco had a distinct sinking feeling that he knew exactly where it had gone.

"Wolverines?" aIdI said, this time hopefully. "Wolverine sandwich? Eat the sandwich?"

"An intruder," Marco said. "You're trying to tell me that there's an unknown intruder in the Complex, aren't you?"

aIdI nodded with a distinct relief. "Bacon! Bacon wolverine sandwich."

Her image glitched momentarily, then vanished. A few

seconds later, all of the lights went out throughout the Complex.

13

Marco had used the radio unit built into his armored chest plate on several occasions in the past during his less than stellar service, but this was the first time he'd had reason to use it since coming to 54174340. He activated it as he quickly threw on the chest plate, but it took him several seconds before he could get anything through other than static. The standard IPA personal comm units distributed among the common grunts were primitive compared to the hyper-beam unit Stonewerth had, and as such they weren't intended for communication more distant than a few kilometers. They were for teams to communicate with each other over short distances, and that was it.

"All members of Zeta Team, come in! This is Glare! We have an emergency! Over!" Given the hiss and crackle that answered him, Marco thought briefly that the interference from the arch was also preventing these units from working. He was only partially right. He got a response back, but it was garbled and hard to hear.

"...that, Glare," the ghost of Stonewerth's voice said. "...unders... said. What's..."

"I said we have an emergency in the Complex! There's something else in here with us!" The comm responded with an especially loud burst of white noise. Marco switched it off, suddenly afraid that it might give his position away to any enemy that might be coming for him. Not that he had any idea what to expect, but he was pretty sure that whatever had come out of the prism was the source of the sudden power outage. Either that, or Hamlet had hit some especially wrong switches when trying to fix aIdI's speech programs. Even if that were the case, aIdI had seemed pretty convinced they weren't alone. There was still a possibility that their mystery visitor was friendly, but until he knew that for sure, Marco had to be prepared to defend himself.

Once he was fully geared up, Marco crouched low and took up a hiding space behind one of the lab tables. As far as he saw it, he had two options right now. He could either stay exactly where he was and keep hidden, or he could leave the room and try to make sure Hamlet was safe. Tactically, the first option was probably the smartest, but his sense of honor would continue to trouble him until he knew exactly where his compatriot was. Hamlet might be hiding himself, or he might be ripped into tiny pieces somewhere. Or he might be *about* to be ripped into pieces, and Marco could be the only one who could prevent it. Once that thought crossed his mind, hiding no longer felt like a viable option.

If Zeta Team had been issued some of the more modern helmets, they would have come with flip-down, holo-tactical readouts that would have allowed Marco to better see in the dark. Instead they had been issued older, no-frills surplus helmets that weren't needed by any of the units that the IPA considered important. Marco was going to have to hope that his vision would adapt enough to the darkness that he could see movement if something came at him. But given the coloring and speed of whatever he'd seen on the holo-feed, he didn't think much of his chances.

He'd been in minor combat situations before, but he'd always had lots of backup during those instances. He'd never truly been afraid. Now, however, he honestly wondered for the first time if he was going to die in some form of combat. This was much different than the sanitized missions he'd been a part of in the past.

Marco did a quick search of the room, poking his rifle in a couple of nooks and crannies, but he highly doubted that any sort of alien life form was in the room with him. Either he would have noticed something was off, or the thing would have already come at him. Still, he tried to be as thorough as possible before getting to the door. Once there, he took a couple of deep breaths to calm himself, then moved out into the Hall.

From here he could go either left or right. Marco took a couple of seconds with his back against the wall to think this through, then, keeping his back covered and his rifle pointed in such a way that he could quickly aim at a threat coming from either side, he slowly sidled to the right. If he'd gone left, he would have passed Weirdlust's and Doc's labs, then been able to reach the main door and easily get out of the Complex. But aIdI's memory core was in one of the storage rooms to the right, so that was where Hamlet would likely be.

His senses were hyper-alert as he constantly scanned his surroundings. He even made sure to consistently look up just in case something was hanging from the ceiling waiting to drop and grab him. The floor was solid enough that he didn't think he had to worry about anything popping up through it, but he was acutely aware that in some places the wall behind was made of a distressingly thin material. If something could somehow sense him through the wall, his imagination easily conjured a nightmare scenario where it would burst through the wall, grab him, and pull him back through before he even had the chance to scream.

At that mental image, he stopped and took a few more deep breaths. His heart hammered and his bladder felt achingly full, like a sufficient scare would result in him pissing himself. If he didn't get a grip on himself, he wasn't going to need some alien being to get him. He would simply have a heart attack and do the creature's job for it.

Marco reached a door and opened it just long enough to peer in. This was one of the storage rooms, but it wasn't where they kept aIdI's core. There could be something in here, but he didn't think he had time to search it. Once he was satisfied that there was nothing immediately beyond the door, he closed it, then, after a moment's thought, pulled out a bullet from his extra ammo and lodged it in the crack under the door. He wasn't sure if that would be enough to keep the door from opening, especially if their mysterious visitor was especially strong, but at the very least he would hear the bullet scraping over the floor if someone tried to get through.

He'd proceeded a couple of meters down the hall before he *did* hear something from back the direction he had come, but it wasn't a door opening. Instead it sounded like it might have been boots stepping as lightly as possible. He probably wouldn't have even heard them if his senses hadn't been on high alert. Marco held his place as he waited for two forms to come out of the darkness. They were nearly on him before they themselves reacted to his presence, and one of them started to swing a rifle in his direction before the other stopped them.

"That's Glare," someone whispered. It was either Thorn or Tulip, but their voices sounded so much alike that Marco couldn't be sure until she got closer. It was only then that he could make out Thorn and Spam in the gloom.

"What's happening?" Spam whispered to him. "Stonewerth sent us in after we all heard the message, but it was garbled."

"She only sent the two of you?" Marco asked.

"Yeah, well, the situation outside has changed," Thorn whispered back. "The two of us were all that she felt safe sparing."

Marco didn't like the sound of that at all, but now was not the time to go into the details. That would have to wait until they'd dealt with any potential threats already inside the Complex.

"Hamlet went to fix aIdI's vocabulary program and he hasn't come back," Marco said. "Before all the power went out, I saw the video feed of the prism before we came out and saw as it changed. Something came out of it. Whatever it was, I think it's in the building."

Thorn took the lead, with Marco in the middle and Spam delicately walking backwards to guard their rear approach. Marco stopped her just before the next door. "aIdI's core and the power supply are both in there." Thorn nodded (or at least Marco thought she did, as it was pretty hard to tell in the darkness), then led them into the storage room. This was one of the larger rooms of the building, but as it was where the bulk of the Complex's various systems were, it was relatively cramped. The three soldiers had to form a straight line in order to get down the corridors between shelves and cabinets. Marco kept Thorn covered as she checked any space around them big enough for a small animal to hide in. Marco guessed that whatever had come out of the prism was much bigger than that, but they had to be thorough. He almost chuckled as it occurred to them that none of them would have been thorough doing anything at all just yesterday. A single day could make all the difference.

Marco smelled the sharp metallic scent of blood in the air before he saw it. As they rounded a corner to reach aIdI's core, Thorn's boots squelched in a thick pool of something. Marco knew Hamlet was dead before they saw the body, but that didn't make the sight any less shocking.

In front of aIdI's core, several circuit boards had been pulled out and set aside. They didn't appear to be damaged, making

Marco think that Hamlet had done that before he'd been killed, and possibly that was what had caused the power outage. It all looked like it could be put together again quite easily, which was far, far better than anyone would have been able to say about Hamlet. He had been pulled apart as well, just with far less care. His limbs were ripped into several pieces each and strewn about the floor. His head had rolled to the side and come to a rest right below a storage shelf full of old cowboy hats.

Why are those even here? Marco wondered, then realized his mind had to be concentrating on that absurd detail purely as a way to keep his mind from losing it over the gruesome tableau in front of them.

The worst damage was to Hamlet's torso. His rib cage had been pried open and his organs removed to be put in a loose pile to the side. A closer look at the organs showed that a single bite had been taken out of each one of them, as though whatever had killed Hamlet had considered him a tasting tray of hors d'oeuvres that it hadn't actually enjoyed that much.

"So much for Tulip's hopes that the prism contained puppies," Thorn whispered. There was a manic note in her voice, as though she were trying not to laugh and scream at the same time.

Spam turned on his comm unit for just a few seconds, risking the loud hiss of static to make sure that he'd relayed the fact that Hamlet was dead, and that if they didn't come out of the Complex within the next ten minutes, the rest of Zeta Team was to assume they were dead and do everything they could to seal the building off. None of them were positive that the whole message had even gone through to the others, but those simple words cemented in Marco's head the gravity of what was going on in a way that nothing else had yet.

There was a hostile force on Planetoid 54174340, and it fully had the ability to completely wipe out the meager force stationed here. They were truly, unequivocally in danger.

That wasn't the way it was supposed to be here.

Marco did his best to force those thoughts out of his head. They were unbecoming of a soldier in the IPA. Now was the time where he had to act exactly like the fighter so much of the brass thought it was impossible for him to be. If Marco didn't do it for himself, then at the very least he had to do it for his comrades. That, after all, is what Colonel Horitz would have done for him.

"I don't know how to put this thing back together," Thorn said as she looked at the pile of circuit boards. "Marco, do you think you can do it and turn the lights back on?"

"Maybe we shouldn't," Spam said. "If we do, that will take away any element of surprise we might have against whatever's in here."

"I'm pretty sure I could do it," Marco said. "Just not quickly. We'd waste too much time trying to do it now. Lights might give us a tactical advantage, but we need to do this all quickly, I think."

"Yeah, especially with the other prisms," Thorn said.

"Other prisms?" Marco asked.

"That's the other thing that's occupying Stonewerth and the others," Spam said. "We'll tell you more about it when we're not in danger of joining poor Hamlet here."

As much as the sight sickened him, Marco took a closer look at the partially-eaten organs. "Very sharp teeth," he said. "Jaw looks slightly bigger than that of a human, so we're probably dealing with something larger than us, but not by much."

"Anything else you can figure out about it just by looking at this mess?" Thorn asked.

"Sure. It's dangerous."

"Thanks, Marco. Very helpful."

Since there obviously wasn't anything they could do for Hamlet anymore, and they had already pretty thoroughly checked the room, the three of them took the quickest path to the exit, then did the bullet trick so they would hear if their adversary tried to backtrack and hide somewhere they'd already checked.

"Well?" Thorn asked quietly once they were back in the hall. "Where should we check next?"

There were still a large number of rooms where they could look, many of them just as crammed with random junk as the ones they had already checked. Yet as Marco thought back to the carnage they had just seen next to aIdI's core, he had an idea what exactly their intruder was looking for.

"The kitchen," Marco whispered. "I think it's looking for food, and apparently Hamlet didn't agree with it."

The closer they got to the kitchen, the more signs they saw that something had been through this area recently. At one point they passed a dent in the thin wall where something had hit it hard, a piece of damage that Marco was pretty sure had not been there before. Once or twice he saw small drops of blood, likely from Hamlet, as well as an oily black substance that Marco didn't want to touch and couldn't quite identify. The most telling sign, though, was the smell they began to pick up right outside the main kitchen door.

Thorn sniffed and scrunched up her nose. "Smells familiar, but I couldn't tell you what it is."

"Petrichor," Spam said.

Thorn gave him a quizzical look.

"That's the name of that thing you smell right before a good rain on Earth," Marco said. "I'm pretty sure you can smell it on a few other planets, too."

"It's got some unpleasant undertones to the scent, however," Spam said. "Like, I don't know, ozone and burnt motor oil."

"Shhh," Marco said, suddenly putting up his hand. He had definitely heard something moving around on the tile floor on the kitchen. It reminded him of the scratching noise of a small dog's claws as it slid around on a freshly polished floor. This noise was a bit louder, though, indicating something much larger than a dog. All three of them made sure their rifles were at the ready as they crouched low and entered the kitchen.

The refrigerator, given its occasional import as a backup cooling unit for unauthorized biological experiments, was hooked up to an emergency battery separate from the main power supply. As such, the open door of the fridge provided them with a small amount of light as they made their way in. The door they'd come in through kept them at an angle where the open fridge door was between them and whatever had invaded their space, so they couldn't immediately see many details. From this angle, they just saw that the thing was pitch black, shiny and oozing something slightly from its back, and slightly taller than Shrug. It was bent low with its head deep in the refrigerator, and judging from the smacking sounds it made, it had finally found some kind of food that agreed with it.

Marco froze and stared at the partially exposed alien creature. Was this really one from the race that had built the gateway? So far, his impression was less of a sophisticated, highly-evolved life form than of a feral predator. He felt an odd combination of awe and disappointment. For the first time ever, humanity was making contact with another sentient species, yet the first thing this species did was kill a human and then make a pig of itself in the scientists' leftovers.

No, not just their leftovers, Marco realized. It would also be eating some of Doc's biological experiments and specimens. And they all knew the effect such a thing had on humans. Marco had no clue whether or not this alien's physiology would react in a similar manner, but if it did then they might have an advantage against it.

Marco nodded at the others, then gestured for them to take flanking positions around the fridge. They moved quietly, yet every moment that the thing didn't hear and realize their presence amazed Marco. It couldn't possibly be that hungry that it ignored all signs that it wasn't alone, could it? Of course, it wasn't like Marco knew when the last time had been that the thing had been able to eat.

That particular detail stuck in his mind. He didn't know what it meant yet, but he filed it away with the knowledge that it would probably be important later.

It suddenly occurred to Marco that, out of all the myriad pieces of knowledge he had received in basic training, none of it had included the proper diplomacy for first contact. If this thing was in fact intelligent, then the slightest misstep could accidentally result in some kind of interstellar war. And given his record, he was the absolute last person the Interplanetary Army wanted in this position. His natural inclination was to take the lead on this, but a crippling doubt came over him. Every human on this planet was considered a screw-up, but he was the biggest screw-up of them all.

He glanced at Thorn, who looked just as much at a loss as Marco. Thankfully, Spam recognized the hesitance of both his comrades. After taking a deep breath, Spam cleared his throat and said, "Excuse me. We're going to have to ask you to please stand still."

The creature stopped moving. Spam looked like he was about to say something else, then apparently realized that the alien creature likely hadn't understood a thing he had said. Spam had said it in as polite and calm a manner as possible, but it would be a mistake to assume that the alien would interpret the tone in the same way a human would. For all any of them knew, the creature might have decided that was the sound of someone calling its mother a whore.

Several more seconds passed in absolute stillness. Not a single thing moved.

Then something tipped over in the fridge. Marco had no idea what it was, nor did it matter. At the sudden intrusion into the quiet, the creature turned on them and, with a high-pitched screech, moved right for Spam.

The violence was quick and ended in less than a couple of seconds. All three soldiers simultaneously fired at the creature, yet even with their trigger-happy reflexes, the alien still managed to get within half a meter of Spam before it collapsed to the floor. Just like that, the silence descended on them again, and all three stood still once more, their rifles pointed at the corpse on the floor just in case it wasn't quite as dead as it appeared.

In the light of the open refrigerator, the three of them now had a better view of the creature that had come out of the prism and killed Hamlet. It was spindly with four long arms and three smaller appendages at the end of each one that could almost but not quite be called fingers. It didn't seem to have any legs. Instead it possessed a single slug-like foot that protruded from the bottom half of its body. From the brief view Marco had gotten during its two seconds of attempted violence, it appeared to propel itself along the floor with the same fluid motions of a snake, yet somehow so much faster. It had something vaguely like a head, but Marco couldn't see any noticeable eyes. It did have a wide, gaping mouth. Something pale blue, probably the creature's equivalent of blood, leaked from all the numerous bullet holes they had put in its body. This fluid mixed with a darker, nearly black-blue ooze that coated its entire body.

"Are we sure it's dead?" Thorn asked quietly. Marco half-expected the creature to suddenly jump up and attack them, but it didn't.

"Pretty sure," Marco said.

"Do you think that's what's going to come out of the others?" Thorn asked Spam.

"Explain?" Marco asked.

"That's the other situation going on that we didn't have time to tell you about," Spam said to him. "While you were in here, three more of the prisms appeared from the gateway. Whatever this thing was," Spam said as he poked it with the end of his rifle, "we're about to get more."

14

There were suddenly a large number of things they felt like they had to do in a short period of time. Hamlet's body had to be taken care of, as did the mysterious alien visitor that now had some of Doc's special mold growing in the blue blood leaking from the side of its mouth. They needed to get aIdI back online, along with the Complex's lights and power, and they had to fix her speech components ASAP if they wanted the AI's help in analyzing everything that had happened so far. But before they could do any of that, they had to get back outside, report what had happened, and make sure that the three new prisms hadn't already released their deadly occupants.

Although Marco didn't have a mirror, he could guess at how terrible he looked based both on the haggard appearance of Thorn and Spam, as well as the deep mental drain. It felt like something had reached into him and tried to pull out a few small pieces of his soul. This, apparently, was what shock felt like when first contact went horribly wrong. The rest of the team gathered around the ruins also looked worried and exhausted, but from their reactions at seeing them come out of the Complex, Thorn, Spam, and Marco had to look much, much worse.

Stonewerth jogged up to join them as soon as they were out of the building. "Status report," she said in a gruff yet calm manner. It was the tone of a true commanding officer, and it was unlike anything Marco had heard come out of her before this.

To Marco's surprise, both Spam and Thorn looked to Marco like they were deferring to him. All three of them were the same rank, and just in terms of seniority Marco should have been the low man in the pile, but somehow the events of the last day had led to him being treated with a sort of grudging respect.

"Hamlet's dead," Marco said. He told about everything he had seen in the Complex, starting with what aIdI had shown him and going all the way through their confrontation with the alien creature. Stonewerth listened to it all wordlessly, nodding occasionally, then gestured for them all to follow her back to the ruins. Tulip and Shrug had pulled some junk from the Hall, mostly unused bed frames, and had created two short makeshift walls behind which they could crouch and keep a good eye on everything within the force field. Doc tentatively followed Stonewerth everywhere she went, chattering nervously to herself in scientific mumbo jumbo. The whole feel of the scene was grim and surreal. Marco had a peculiar feeling like an invisible cloud had come over all of them, and if he breathed it in too much, it might choke him to death. It was both oppressive and depressing.

As Stonewerth switched Thorn and Spam out for the other two so that she could brief them on everything that had gone down in the Complex, Marco moved a little closer to the force field so he could see the three new arrivals. The original prism had crumbled into dust by now, and Weirdlust's body beneath the pile of ash looked like it was fast going that way as well. The three new prisms looked exactly as the original had just after it had come out of the gateway. Whatever process that first had gone through, apparently something was keeping these from doing the same.

"It was like the first had sucked the moisture out of Weirdlust," Marco said, more to himself than anyone else, although when he looked around he saw that Doc at least was within hearing distance and listened despite her soft litany of technical jargon. "That's what allowed it to release the creature that had been inside. But there's no nearby moisture for the new ones to absorb. So we should be safe from these, right?" That logic felt like it should have been right, but a sense of dread and unease continued to grow, forming a black cloud over his senses that made it hard for him to think. The feeling was strange, like there would never be joy again, much like when he had gone through his depressive episode earlier in the month. Maybe that temporary madness was coming back to him. If so, Marco couldn't think of a worse time, and that only drained at his will even more.

On some level, Marco felt his special sense for details trying to tell him something important, and yet it just wouldn't come. Something was wrong.

Somewhere nearby, he thought he heard someone speaking French. Tulip. She was having another one of her Joan of Arc episodes. Thorn, from her station at the defensive wall, had noticed this and was busy cursing out her sister in a rather vile string of angry words. Stonewerth heard this and lost it, yelling at Thorn to drop and give her a thousand immediately. Thorn told her where to shove it, which only made Stonewerth angrier.

Marco turned to Spam and saw him staring strangely at his own arm. It was the kind of look a starving man might give a steak.

Focus, Marco thought. *Something is happening. I need to concentrate. I need to figure it out. It's what I do.* But he couldn't. It felt like something was blocking his own thoughts, and that only made him slide deeper into despair. It blossomed into full-on self-loathing as he realized what an utter failure he must seem like to Colonel Horitz. He could image the man that had been like his father glaring down at him disapprovingly, his voice calm even as he told Marco that he was a disgrace, that it was a good thing that his mother was already dead because otherwise she would die of shame at the shambles Marco had made of his life. Marco felt tears begin to run down his cheeks as he felt an overwhelming need to drop to his knees and then assume a fetal position on the ground.

Shrug ran up to Marco and slapped him in the face.

Marco saw stars for several moments. When his senses started to come back, his first impulse was to hit Shrug right back. Then he saw the worried yet determined look in Shrug's eyes. For the briefest of moments, Marco's head felt clear. That dark fog began to creep back into his brain soon after, but not so quickly that his gift didn't kick in and force him to take another long look at his surroundings.

Spam had actually started chewing on his arm. He probably would have already ripped out a chunk of his own flesh if it weren't for the fact that his uniform had long sleeves. Thorn was screaming obscenities at Stonewerth, who had stopped trying to get Thorn to do her one thousand pushups and instead had dropped to the ground to do them herself. Doc was running around measuring random things with a measuring tape that didn't actually exist, murmuring to herself that everything around her seemed to be shrinking and growing by itself in defiance of the laws of physics and this wouldn't do and maybe she could just get someone to strip for her so she could get a baseline reading. In the middle of this small pocket of chaos, Tulip stood in a heroic pose while holding an imaginary sword over her head as she commanded an imaginary army to storm an imaginary castle.

Marco shook his head, trying to physically dislodge the gray fog from his brain. "Shrug, what's going on?"

Shrug, of course, shrugged. Then, with great concentration, he too shook his head, then pointed in the direction of the three stone prisms. The symbols on them were glowing and pulsing more wildly now, like they were getting ready to discharge something. But that couldn't be, Marco thought. There was no moisture for them to absorb.

Unless moisture wasn't the only thing they could absorb to do what they needed to do. Maybe they had other ways of releasing their occupants.

Like, say, draining sanity and causing madness all around them.

Suddenly everything else Marco had seen of his fellow team members over the last month took on a new meaning. Everyone had always just assumed that the madness of this place was caused by the boredom and the isolation. No one had ever stopped to think that the ruins themselves might be causing it. With the gateway in pieces, maybe they hadn't been able to do the job effectively enough to do what they were supposed to. But now?

Marco fought back the crippling malaise that threatened to take over him and instead concentrated on Shrug. "Why isn't this affecting you?" he asked.

Shrug paused halfway through a shrug before he shook his head, then pointed at his mask. Marco could only guess at the meaning. Whatever particular form the madness was trying to take in Shrug, it might have had a major verbal component. But since Shrug couldn't talk, it wasn't able to take the strong hold of him that it did to the others.

That was just conjecture, though. Marco would have to ask Shrug to write down the full reason later. For now, it looked like they were running out of time before the prism stones released more of the oily black terrors. "What... what do you want me to do?" Marco managed to ask.

Shrug pointed at all the weird chaos happening around them,

then made a motion like he was grabbing Marco by the arms and shaking him. He followed this with a pantomime of slapping Marco before shrugging one last time. Then he hefted his rifle and pointed it at the prisms.

"I think I understand," Marco said. He still felt groggy and ready to topple over in tears over who knew what. He thought he understood Shrug's meaning, though. Shrug took up a position where he would easily be able to shoot at any of the creatures if they came out of the stones and went directly for him, while Marco stumbled over to Spam. Spam had managed to get through most of his sleeve and had finally drawn his own blood, although it didn't yet look like the wound was deep. Marco grabbed him by the shoulder and shook him.

"Spam, you've got to stop," Marco said. "It's the prisms. They're doing this to you. Most people from your planet aren't really cannibals, remember?"

Spam turned and looked at him. For several moments there didn't appear to be any recognition in his eyes. There was just something feral, savage, uncontrollable. Spam gnashed his teeth, forcing Marco to take a step back.

"Well, let's see if this works," Marco mumbled to himself. With all the force he could muster, he smacked Spam across the face. Spam's head snapped to the side before he looked right back at Marco with an even more savage expression than before.

"Okay, bad idea," Marco said. Spam launched himself at Marco, knocking him onto his back and leaving him prone as Spam bent lower as though he were about to take a chomp out of Marco's neck. Right before he did, though, Spam pulled back, and Marco could see some of the humanity returning to his eyes.

"Whu... whu?" Spam sputtered. Marco didn't have the time to try explaining it to him. He pushed Spam off himself, then looked at the prisms. One had stopped pulsing, and the blackness covered it as it prepared to release another of the alien creatures.

"Spam, get your rifle and focus on what's about to come out at us!" Marco yelled. He didn't stop to see if Spam did as he was told. Instead he quickly assessed his surroundings and decided that Thorn was the least far gone of the remaining team members stuck in their madness. He tried a similar technique on her, thankfully not having to go so far as smacking her before she started to come back to her senses. Marco had a feeling that, if he'd been forced to try, she would have smacked back with far more violence than Marco could manage.

"Holy shit, here it comes!" Spam cried out. Marco looked to see that the first prism had discharged its passenger, but unlike the one Marco had seen on the video feed, this one didn't immediately dart off. It stopped in front of the already deteriorating prism, and despite its apparent lack of eyes, it seemed to be watching and gauging the reactions of the humans in front of it.

"What's it doing?" Thorn asked. She still had a hazy, angry look to her, but Marco couldn't tell if that was a residual effect of her madness or if she was just plain mad as hell that she'd fallen under its sway. Marco didn't know the answer to her question, but he saw in the alien a very different demeanor than the one they'd confronted in the kitchen. That one had seemed like a wild animal. This one was calculating. It showed evidence of intelligence, of thought. It was taking in everything around it and, possibly, formulating a plan.

The darkness started to grow over the second and third prisms. Unlike the first time, the team knew what was going to happen and was prepared to shoot the creatures the instant they left the protection of the force field. But they still only had two people with their weapons at the ready, and three more people trapped in their own delusions that might prove to be a liability in a sudden fight.

"Thorn, see if you can get Doc, Tulip, and Stonewerth to snap out of it," Marco said. "We're going to need everyone we can in order to keep those things from getting loose." Thorn promptly went over to her sister and commanded her to wake up, although she screamed it in French. Marco made sure his rifle was ready for an attack, then joined Shrug and Spam.

The two remaining prisms released their aliens. Both of them looked for a second like they were going to rush out through the force field and attack, but before they could, they responded to some kind of signal only they could sense from the first creature. They turned to look at it, obviously offering it deference. The first one from this batch had to be a leader of some kind. Marco scanned it for anything he might be able to use to uniquely identify it among the others. In almost all ways it was the same as the one they'd confronted in the Complex, but it was shorter than the other two around it. Marco got the impression that this was a detail he would need to remember. To himself, he identified the smaller one as Fearless Leader then, his mind catching on some half-remembered bit of pop culture trivia from long ago, decided that the names of the other two would be Boris and Natasha.

"What are they doing?" Spam asked.

"Strategy," Marco said. "They're making plans."

"The one in the kitchen didn't act like it was making any plans," Spam said.

"Well, obviously Fearless Leader is different," Marco said. Spam raised an eyebrow at the name, but he apparently understood which one Marco was talking about.

Behind them, Thorn didn't seem to be having a lot of luck bringing the others back to reality. Tulip kept screaming the word "Feu!" as though she were in mortal pain, Stonewerth was on pushup two-hundred and five, and Doc was now trying to get Thorn to strip so she could measure the size of her breasts. Marco didn't think any of them were going to be of any help, and from the increased rage in Thorn's voice, it sounded like she was falling back under the spell as well. Marco himself felt like a heavy weight was coming down on his mind, reminding him that he was a failure, that he could never amount to anything, that the best thing to do might be to turn his rifle on himself and pull the trigger. Spam was getting that hungry look in his eyes again. Only Shrug didn't seem much different than normal. What little could be seen of his face showed a distinct amount of worry, but whatever was trying to take hold in his mind, he was the one fighting it the best.

"Shrug," Marco muttered. His arms felt too heavy for him to keep his weapon raised. "You have to… you have to be the one that…" Marco dropped to his knees and started sobbing.

Even through this, though, he kept enough concentration that he saw everything that happened next.

Fearless Leader made no noise, nor any gesture, but somehow it sent the word to Boris and Natasha that now was the time to attack. Marco didn't know if it could understand the exact nature of what was happening to the humans (hell, Marco couldn't even be one hundred percent certain himself), but it obviously realized that most of the defenders were incapacitated. Shrug twitched slightly in his spot, probably a sign that he was fighting off his own internal demons. It wasn't enough to slow down his reflexes, though, and the instant Boris and Natasha were beyond the force field, he started firing. He hit Natasha full on in the abdomen, which slowed her down but didn't completely stop her, while Boris dashed to the side and came at Shrug from an angle. Shrug turned and aimed at Boris, but it was too fast. With all four arms it raked its fingers across Shrug's face, sending blood and bits of flesh flying.

"No," Spam said hoarsely. He struggled to tear his eyes away from the gash in his arm, trying to take aim at the alien. Marco did likewise, but the thing ripped into Shrug again before either of them could fire. As Shrug hit the ground in a bloody mess, both Spam and Marco squeezed their triggers and sent a storm of bullets into the creature. Much like the one in the Complex, Boris erupted in a shower of blue blood. They kept firing for longer than they probably needed, but Marco honestly had trouble stopping, given the gray fog clouding his brain. He only ceased firing when he realized that the creature had fallen on top of Shrug's prone body, and any further attempt to shoot it would only hit Shrug.

Spam stood up straight, his eyes now clear. Marco felt his own mind clearing, and as he looked around it looked like everyone else was feeling the same way. Stonewerth had stopped her needless pushups, instead getting to her knees as she blinked at the scene around her. Tulip and Thorn had stopped screaming at each other, and while Doc was still eyeing Thorn's breasts as though they were the ultimate scientific curiosities, at least she was no longer trying to strip anyone. The whole mood was almost tranquil following the bizarre chaos Marco had just seen. It was almost enough to make him forget that there was still one more alien with them on this side of the force field. Almost.

Natasha had taken just enough damage from Shrug that it must have decided to cut its losses and run, but it didn't have the same speed it had evidenced earlier. Instead it was trying to crawl back in the direction of Fearless Leader. The instant it touched the force field, the creature gave a shriek at the shock and pulled away, toppling over, stunned, next to one of the poles. Fearless Leader, for its part, did nothing. It simply continued to somehow observe in its sightless way. It made no attempt to cross the force field, nor did it seem overly concerned about the fate of its two companions. Marco couldn't help but wonder what it was thinking, then decided that he probably didn't want to know.

As the other members of the team rushed to Shrug, Marco took notice of the other events within the force field. The three prisms continued their crumbling, but that was not nearly so interesting as the way the gateway once again looked like it was preparing to release more prisms. It was the prisms, Marco thought, that had been most responsible for all of them losing it, and given the way Marco, Thorn, and Spam hadn't shown any symptoms of their madness until they had approached the gateway again, distance had to in some way affect how and why the insanity took over them. If the gateway released more and they were still standing out here when it happened, he doubted they would all be able to fight off their inner demons long enough to stop another attack. They couldn't be here when the next set of prisms came through.

"We've got to go," Marco said. "We should all get back to the Complex. We can lock all the entrances."

Stonewerth looked up at him and nodded, then turned her attention back to Shrug. "You hear that, buddy? We've got a plan. Maybe there's something we can do to save ourselves. And we have you to thank for that, do you understand?"

Marco finally came close enough to get through the loose circle of people surrounding Shrug and get a good look. Shrug didn't move, nor did he look like he would ever be able to move again. His face, already half-ravaged by that long ago explosion, was now completely gone. If not for his unusual height and the shredded remains of his mask, Marco wouldn't have even been able to identify him. His chest was ripped open similar to what they had found with Hamlet, but this time Boris hadn't had the time to do anything with the guts.

Shrug most definitely wasn't capable of hearing Stonewerth as she said a few gentle words of good-bye to her friend, but no one would dare tell her that. Once Stonewerth appeared to be finished, she stood up and nodded in the direction of Natasha.

"Tulip and Thorn, take care of that thing with extreme vengeance. And make sure the remaining one gets a good look at what we do to those that harm us, if it even can look at anything."

The sisters did as they were told. They were quick and efficient, but they made no effort to hide their execution from the remaining alien. Fearless Leader, for its part, gave no indication that it cared. Once that was taken care of, Stonewerth pointed in the direction of the Complex. "You all heard Glare. We need to get out of here before whatever that was happens to us again. Make sure every door in and out of that place is barricaded. It looks like we're about to be in for some kind of siege."

She stooped down and gently took Shrug's body in her arms. Although she was stocky, it didn't look like she should have been able to carry the overly-tall man's remains. Several of the others offered to help, yet Stonewerth silently shook them all off. Apparently she thoroughly believed this was her job and hers alone.

And through it all, as they made their hasty retreat, Fearless Leader stayed completely still in its spot within the circle of force fields, observing everything.

15

The first two things that had to be done in the Complex, before any of them could try making sense of everything that had happened so far, were to secure all the entrances as well as get aIdI and the power back online. The doors were fairly easy. Stonewerth, Spam, and the twins merely had to go to each one and engage the emergency siege locks. The only problem there was that no one had ever had a reason to activate the siege locks before, so there was some confusion as to how they even operated. The siege locks put down an extra steel barrier over each exit and were supposed to be triggered from the computer system. The manual controls all still worked, at least, even if all of them were stiff and hard to operate thanks to years of neglect and disuse.

aIdI and the power were a different story. Marco and Doc, as the only ones with anything resembling technical know-how, were forced to scour through the circuit boards and put them all back, not even in the place they had been before but rather in such a way that aIdI's vocals would be corrected. They couldn't risk anymore miscommunications, after all. The previous one had contributed to Hamlet's death, and the number of team members, already dangerously low before all this had started, was still dwindling. Little things like that could get more people killed. Between the two of them, however, Doc and Marco managed to have everything back up and running shortly after the others had secured the facility.

So now they had a locked building, an AI to help them sort this all out, power, and what little weaponry they'd brought with them after retreating from the gateway. All that was left was to figure out just what the hell to do next.

"First thing's first," Stonewerth said once they were all back in one place again. As Doc was the only official scientist left, and they would likely be needing her expertise, they all gathered in her claustrophobically cramped lab. "From this point on, no more splitting up. Period."

"Are you sure that's a good idea?" Thorn asked. "There might be things we can get done quicker if we have several groups."

"There's only six of us," Stonewerth said. "And we still don't know how many of those aliens there's going to be by the time the gateway is finished spitting them out, if it ever finishes at all. Several groups might be able to get one or two things done faster, but they can also be picked off quicker."

"So what's the plan, then?" Spam asked. "Do we even have one?"

"No, so we better fricking come up with one quick," Stonewerth said. "Anyone got any ideas on where to start?"

"The alien in the kitchen," Doc said. "If we go and get it to study it in here, I might be able to find some things out about them that could help us. Weaknesses, and things like that."

"And now that aIdI's back to working the way she should, we can further study the gateway," Marco said. "Maybe we can find out exactly what it is and what it's doing."

"I think it's pretty obvious what it's doing," Thorn said. "It's the portal for an invasion force."

"We can't assume that," Tulip said.

"Sis, I love you," Thorn said, "but if you still try to say it will eventually give us puppies, I swear to God that I'm going to…"

"No, she's right," Marco said.

Tulip looked surprised. "About the puppies?"

"About the fact that we can't assume this is some kind of invasion."

"What the hell else could it be?" Spam asked.

"I don't know, but as far as an invasion, it doesn't seem to be a very tactical one so far, does it?" Marco asked. "First the gateway sends one through, and that needs special conditions for the prism to get unlocked and the passenger to get out. Then three, also needing special conditions."

"Alright, hold it for a second," Stonewerth said. "Before we go any further, do you have any idea what just happened back there? The special conditions, I mean. Why did we all start freaking from out of nowhere?"

"We didn't," Marco said. "It's been making us slowly lose it for a long time. Whatever technology was causing it, it's been leaking out of the ruins probably for as long as humans have been here. We all just thought we were having various psychological problems because of the nature of our post. Apparently it takes whatever insecurities or delusions we already have and amplifies them. And somehow, don't ask me how exactly, it can take that madness and use it like a power source. For the first one, it used the moisture from Weirdlust. However the technology works, that must be a more effective energy source. When the next prisms didn't have anything like that in the immediate vicinity, however, it went to that secondary method."

Marco cocked his head and thought about this for a second. "Come to think of it, that might explain part of why the gateway could reassemble itself with only minimal effort from Weirdlust and Hamlet. Humans have been on 54174340 for almost a century now. At first, when there were lots of people, the madness the ruins caused was minimal because there were so many people and it only had to take a little bit from each. As the number of people dwindled and the amount of times those people had to stay increased, the more noticeable it all became. We just interpreted it as the fragile human psyche cracking under pressure."

"So you're saying the reason I'm Joan of Arc is because the ruins turned me into her?" Tulip asked.

"Uh, close enough, yeah," Marco said. "Did you maybe have some kind of obsession with her before you came here?"

"Yeah, I always loved stories about her."

"Then the ruins must have amplified the obsession. That's why all of us are a little bit battier than one would expect," Marco said. "Stonewerth feels guilty about not keeping us up to military standards, so she occasionally goes off on us like a drill instructor. Doc is obsessed with science and sex, so… yeah, there's that. I feel guilty and insecure about the incidents that put me here…"

Stonewerth hissed and nodded. "That's why the woman you replaced here on the planetoid suddenly became sexually abusive, I'm betting."

"Probably, yes. There was already something there. Go back far enough in the records and I'm sure you'll find a lot more of this. All of it was like the ruins trying to charge a battery, a battery that would eventually power it enough to put it all back together. Weirdlust and Hamlet just gave it the final push. Given a little more time, it probably would have put itself back together without their help. They didn't really do anything wrong. All of this would have happened eventually."

"Okay then," Stonewerth said. "Go back to why you don't think this is an invasion. Because you still haven't convinced me."

"Honestly, I'm not exactly convinced myself," Marco said. "But if humans were trying to do some kind of invasion, they wouldn't do it piecemeal like this. Even if the aliens have completely different psychologies and ways of thinking, they would have to realize that this would be ineffective."

"That still doesn't tell us anything about what it would be instead, though," Spam said.

"You know what it reminds me of?" Tulip asked. "A convenience store."

Everyone stared at her for several seconds before turning back to Marco. "Anyway," Marco started. "As I was saying…"

"Wait. I know that sounds stupid, but hear me out," Tulip said. "Have any of you guys ever had to work in a convenience store?"

"Convenience stores aren't exactly common on a planet famous for food shortages," Spam said grudgingly.

"It's what Thorn and I did before we joined the IPA," Tulip said. "We worked there for extra cash, but it wasn't enough to support our family, so we joined up and started sending our paychecks back to Mom and Dad."

"I don't see where you're going with this, though, sis," Thorn said. "How the hell is this making you think of those hellish years when we had to work at the OneStop Mart?"

"Thorn, don't you remember the time delay safes?"

Thorn looked for a second like she still didn't understand what her sister was getting at. Then, slowly, a thoughtful look began to cross Thorn's face.

"Maybe," Thorn said cautiously. "I suppose I could see where you're going with this."

"Then please enlighten the rest of us," Stonewerth said, "because we're all still lost."

"A time delay safe is where businesses like that drop in any kind of large paper bills or valuables," Thorn said. "You don't see them as much anymore except on worlds that still use paper money. Any money that the workers aren't planning on immediately using gets put in a slot. To deter robbers, the safe takes something like ten minutes or so to open. You put in the access code, then it counts down for that time."

"What would be the point of that?" Spam asked.

"The point is that a robber doesn't want to sit around for ten minutes waving a gun at the worker when a cop could show up at any minute," Tulip said. "If a store has a sign saying their extra money is kept in a time delay safe, then a robber is less likely to target that store. Even if they do, they're probably not going to get away with anything more than what little is in the registers."

Spam snorted. "Registers. Safes. Yeah, none of that stuff exists on Lewis-and-Clark. Those would require people to actually have money."

"I still don't see what any of that has to do with what's happening here," Stonewerth said. "Unless you're trying to say that these creatures are some kind of currency, but that's just stupid."

The more Marco had been listening to all this, the more he'd seen where they were going with it. "No, they're not saying we're fighting some kind of alien money, Stonewerth. But they are saying that the gateway is some kind of safe."

"Okay, at this point I officially feel like the dumbest person in the room," Stonewerth said, "and it's pissing me off. If someone here doesn't stop talking in riddles and just flat out tell me what you're all thinking, I'm going to have all of you drop and give me a hundred. And that's not that crazy brain crap talking, this time. You're just annoying me."

"Think about it," Doc said. She, too, had apparently come to the same conclusion as the others, and it visibly excited her. "What's another word for a safe where you put living things?"

Stonewerth cocked her head. "A zoo?"

Spam hissed in a sharp breath as he got it as well. "No, sentient living things. Living things that can think. Living things that maybe you don't want running around."

Stonewerth snorted. "That one's easy. We just call it Planetoid Shithead." She stopped, and suddenly it dawned on her. "The place where you put your unwanted types. The misfits. The screw-ups.

The... the criminals."

Marco nodded. "It's a prison. For the last hundred years, ever since humans discovered the ruins, we thought maybe they'd been left behind on accident, that the stones had fallen apart due to the ravages of time. But they were put that way on purpose as a lock. The ruins, the technology behind them, probably even the oddities in the planet's atmosphere and gravity, all of it exists to create the prison for some kind of ancient alien race that probably vanished on us a long time ago."

"Well, if this alien race is gone, wouldn't the prisoners have died by now?" Tulip asked.

"If it were a prison in the way that humans do it, then sure," Marco said. "But this race was obviously far beyond us. The creatures from their own race that they imprisoned, I bet they were kept in some kind of stasis. That's what each of those prisms are. They're individual cells. By virtue of humans being on 54174340 this whole time, we've accidently been providing the key that slowly opened the gates. The cells are being released a few at a time."

"What's the reason for doing it like that, though?" Spam asked.

"Who knows?" Marco said. "We can't assume that the aliens used the same type of logic that we do, or maybe there's just aspects of the technology we can't understand. Maybe they're being released in small groups to make them more manageable to take care of by whatever would have once served this place as prison guards. Either way, they're being released." Marco paused again. "Names," he said. "Signatures."

"You've lost us again," Tulip said.

Doc, however, understood. "That's what the symbols are. They're like a registry of the prisoners, or prisoner numbers."

"Each one done in the individual prisoner's version of their handwriting or alphabet," Marco said with a nod.

Stonewerth grimaced. "And exactly how many different sets of symbols did you say you found?"

"Just under two hundred," Doc said.

"So that means we're going to have to deal with two hundred of these things?" Tulip asked.

"We're not going to be able to survive that!" Spam said. "We're already down thirty percent of our team, and that's only with four of the creatures released so far!"

Marco turned to the holo-generator near the wall of Doc's lab. "aIdI, are you all finished rebooting by now?"

aIdI's blocky avatar appeared before them. "Affirmative."

"Wow, that's weird," Doc said. "I think that's the first time I've ever heard her actually say that word."

aIdI turned to Doc with a posture that looked suspiciously annoyed. "I could continue to say 'neck tie' if you prefer?"

Stonewerth snorted. "Not only did you guys restore her proper vocabulary, it also looks like you somehow gave her an attitude as well."

"We're glad to have you back up, aIdI," Marco said. "Can you give us a current security display of what the gateway looks like?"

"Anything for you, Glare," she said. Marco tried not to look surprised. Was it just him, or had the AI just tried to flirt with him? It was amazing how much had gotten lost in the translation from aIdI's real words to the nonsense she'd been spouting earlier.

aIdI's avatar was replaced by a holographic view of the gateway. Fearless Leader still stood in more or less the same place. The major difference on the scene, however, were the new prisms.

"Nine of them," Stonewerth said quietly. "We are officially outnumbered."

"Ten if you include the other one," Spam said. "What did you call him, Marco? Fearless Leader?"

"Hey, don't go assuming it's a he," Thorn said. "For all we know that's a she."

"Or for all we know, they don't have gender," Marco said. "Or they have three genders. Or fourteen. We really can't make too many assumptions about anything with them."

"He, she, they, doesn't matter," Stonewerth said. "They all want to kill us."

"Maybe not," Spam said. "Some of them could be non-violent. Like the equivalent of peaceful political prisoners."

Marco thought back to the one they'd killed in the kitchen and the way it had reacted with such unthinking savagery. "That could be the case, for all we know," Marco said. "But I don't think it matters. Think for a moment about how long they've been trapped in there."

"At least a hundred years," Thorn said. "Although probably much, much longer."

"Long enough that we've been finding small bits and pieces of these aliens on other worlds long before we found Shithead," Tulip said.

"So they could have been trapped in their prison for time out of mind, for all we know," Marco said. "Tell me, what would happen to you if you were trapped in a prison for millennia?"

"We'd lose it," Thorn said. "Completely batshit. Kind of like us here, except they don't have something intentionally making them crazy."

"But is that true?" Spam asked. "If the gateway and the prisms have that maddening effect on us when we get too close, isn't it possible that they might have the same effect on someone that's actually trapped inside?"

"Probably even more-so," Marco said. "So what we're going to be dealing with here shortly is right around two hundred alien prisoners, many of them probably violent even before getting locked away, that have been trapped for an extremely long time in something that causes madness."

"So you're saying it doesn't matter if they were peaceful once," Stonewerth said.

"They're not going to be now," Thorn said.

"But we don't actually have to deal with that many, right?" Tulip asked. "They only get out if the prisms have moisture or our brains to feed on."

Doc shook her head and pointed at one of the prisms in the holo-feed. "There's got to be something else they can use to release their prisoners. See right here? This one's pulsing is out of sync with the others. It's going to hatch pretty soon."

"Hatch?" Stonewerth asked.

Doc shrugged. "Seemed like an appropriate word to me."

"So they're still going to get out," Spam said. "One way or the other. It's just that if we go out there, they'll hatch even sooner."

"And the gateway looks like it's priming up to release some more," Thorn said. "We've got to do something. The longer we wait, the worse the odds against us become."

"Except we *can't* do anything," Tulip said. "Not as long as the force field is in place."

"I think that's what Fearless Leader was up to," Marco said. "He or she used the other two to test the abilities of the force field. Now that FL knows how it works, all they need to do is wait for a sufficient group to gather inside the field and then send them all out after us. We'll get overwhelmed."

"Doc, have you found anything yet in the various notes about taking down that force field?" Stonewerth said. "Because to me, it looks like that thing is the main reason they have an advantage over us. If it were gone, we might be able to find a way to even the odds."

"I did find some info. The generator poles had almost a full charge last I saw them used," Doc said. "Since they're designed to help withstand sieges, it could be months before their power goes down by themselves. And, of course, it would be a major design flaw if some attacking force could just switch them off."

"What else might take them out?" Marco asked.

Doc shrugged. "I don't know." Then she stopped and thought about it for a second. "They only work when they're in alignment. If one were to be in the ground at too much of an angle, it wouldn't be able to complete the energy circuit and the field would go down. But again, they're designed to prevent that. You can't just go up to the poles and shove them out of alignment. Once they're planted in the ground, they anchor themselves pretty good. It would take a significant amount of force to push one out of alignment."

"Do we even have anything that could cause that kind of force?" Spam asked.

"Maybe we can find something among the century's worth of junk here in the Complex," Marco said. "But I think, sooner or later, the prisms will do that for us. They get ejected out of the gateway with a great deal of speed. And if you look here…" Marco stopped and pointed at the prisms in the holo-image. "…when they come out, they seem to make a pattern that prevents them from hitting each other, or any of the places where previous ones were ejected. Eventually they're going to have to spread out so far that they will hit one of the poles. Once that happens, the aliens' protection is going to be gone."

Stonewerth snorted. "Fat lot of good that's going to do us. By that point, there will be too many for us to take out."

"It's too bad the comm equipment isn't in the Complex," Doc said. "We could use it to at least tell Command what's happening here, even if they wouldn't be able to reach us in time."

"What good would that do?" Thorn asked. "As long as the gateway is emitting its interference, the comm equipment is little more to us than an anchor."

"Not so," Stonewerth said. "That's what Doc and I were trying to work on when we got Glare's distress signal earlier. We think we have a way to send a message out."

"That's great!" Marco said. "You found a way to make the hyper-space beam work?"

"No, that's still borked. It still starts over after a certain amount of completion," Stonewerth said. "But remember, that's not the only comm equipment we have over there. There was also all the junk that had been blocking the door."

Spam made a disgusted face. "Does that outdated junk even still work?"

"It should," Doc said. "It's just going to be slower to reach them, and slower for us to get a response. Days at the earliest. But it's better than the current option."

"We didn't have time to put it all back together, though," Stonewerth said. "We probably still have about half an hour of work to go on it before we'll know for sure if it works."

"None of which is relevant," Thorn said, "considering the comm equipment is all in the Hall, while we're stuck in here."

Marco watched on the screen as the prism he'd indicated earlier turned black and emitted another creature. It immediately stopped and went to stand by next to Fearless Leader. Several other prisms looked like they were getting ready to hatch as well, and the gateway itself had begun another cycle to set loose more.

"We're running out of time," Marco said. "If we're going to work this problem, we need to get going on it now."

"Keep talking like that, kid, and we may actually make a real soldier out of you yet," Stonewerth said with a smile. Then she turned to look at the others. "Okay everyone. You heard the sergeant. Doc and Glare are taking point on this. Ask them what you need to do and then do it."

Marco gave Stonewerth a puzzled expression. "Major, I'm a private, not a sergeant."

"You are now. I'm giving you a battle promotion. So far I think you've earned it. Now it's time for you to prove that you can keep it."

16

They moved the alien from the kitchen to a table in Doc's lab where she could easily dissect it, then cleared a space in a far corner where they could do their best to give Hamlet and Shrug a temporary resting place. After that, Marco got to work studying all the images he could of the gateway. The rest kept a close eye on the lab's entrance, knowing that at any time Fearless Leader could decide it had enough of a tactical advantage to go on the offensive.

Marco furiously went over all the data he could find, trying to read everything, see everything, interpret everything. While Stonewerth had intended his promotion as a show of confidence and merit, it only made Marco more worried that he would screw up. Someone actually believed in him now, adding a level of pressure he hadn't known before. There had to be something in all the information they had gathered about the gateway so far that would allow them all to stay alive, and the general consensus now seemed to be that he was the only one who could find it.

He just hoped this wouldn't be yet another hat or chicken incident. Unlike those times, however, it wouldn't be chickens dying. It would be the entire human population of 54174340.

Spam wandered over to him. "Marco, relax."

Marco snorted. "There's no time to relax. Didn't you see how many prisms the gateway released this last time? Twenty-seven, and none of them hit the generator poles yet. Yet somehow the prisms are still being powered by something, because they keep hatching."

"I know all that. But I also have seen the way your little gift for details works. Right now, you're doing it wrong."

"Excuse me? Spam, no offense, but that's bullshit. I'm pretty sure I know how I do what I do better than anyone else."

"No Marco, that's the bullshit. If you knew how it worked and how to control it, you wouldn't have ended up in this God-forsaken pit, and you know it. But during all that time you were sitting at the ruins and staring at them, what were you thinking?"

Marco shrugged. "I wasn't really thinking at all."

"Right. And any time at all where you've gotten your gift to work correctly for you, were you ever thinking it through?"

Marco started to understand where Spam was going with this. "No. I wasn't."

"And every time you try to intentionally use it, what happened?"

Despite himself, Marco had to smile. "Chicken incidents."

"Right. So take my advice: go back over all the stuff you've just gone over. But this time, instead of looking for connections, just see it all. Your brain will do its thing and fill in the rest."

"Huh. Thanks, Spam."

Spam patted him on the shoulder. "You've got this." He then went back to his post.

Marco took a deep breath, then went back to where he'd begun.

He was only partially aware when, some unknown time later, Doc spoke up. While he did listen to what she said, all of Marco's focus stayed on the flashing data before him.

"So I don't have sophisticated enough equipment here to be sure of anything, but I've got a few educated guesses," Doc said. The rest of the soldiers, with the exception of Stonewerth who stayed behind to keep an eye on the door, went over to her and gathered around the alien corpse.

"Doc, it looks like you've got this thing's blood all over you," Tulip said. "Are you sure that's a good idea?"

"It tested negative for all known toxins, viruses, and bacteria that are harmful to humans," Doc said.

"Yeah, but what if it, I don't know, turns acidic or something and melts you?"

"Acidic? Why the hell would blood be acidic?" Doc asked.

"Ignore my sister," Thorn said. "She watched too many old holos. Just tell us what you've found."

"Well, to start with, these creatures are invertebrates, but with a cardio-vascular system unlike anything I've ever seen before."

"I didn't understand a word of that," Tulip said.

"She means that they have no back bone and they breathe funny," Spam said.

"An inelegant way to put it, but correct," Doc said.

"Wait, invertebrates?" Stonewerth said from her position at the door. "You mean they're some kind of insects?"

"Not in any way that we would recognize them, but they're close," Doc said. "The top half of the creature has elements we associate with insects or crustaceans, such as an exoskeleton, but the bottom half more closely resembles a mollusk, something like a slug or a snail. Between those two halves are a number of organs I have been unable to identify yet, but since it doesn't have a noticeable heart or lungs, I believe something in there must take their place."

"What's all that smelly black stuff?" Tulip said, pointing at the ooze that still covered the alien's body.

"That, I think, may be proof that Glare is at least partially right about these creatures having gone mad. From what I can tell, that's evidence of cellular degeneration, a sludge that is forming from the basic building blocks of its body breaking down. We saw such a thing on the others as well. My guess is that they weren't supposed to exist in their prison for that long. My expertise is biology, not physics, so I can't say for sure, but whatever weird quantum mechanics are at work in the gateway, they don't play well with biological matter. Maybe it would have been fine if these things had been incarcerated for whatever time had originally been intended, but getting left behind for millennia? It's wrecked them."

While all that was fascinating, Marco's concentration pulled away from what Doc was saying. He'd just found something. He knew it. Somewhere in all that material he'd been absorbing, he had the answer. Yet it was still buried in his subconscious, waiting to come to the surface.

"Quick, someone ask me a question," Marco said. "Anything having to do with our situation."

"Why?" Thorn asked.

"Just do it," Marco responded.

"Okay, then," Thorn said. "Are we all going to die?"

"No," Marco responded instantly. "Not all of us." The answer surprised him as much as anyone. Minutes earlier, he would have hedged his answer. Now, however, he felt strangely certain. He remembered the picture in Horitz's office, the way he had taken in all the details but hadn't interpreted them into anything until he'd been told to talk about them. "Keep asking. I think that might be how it works. My brain's like a calculator. The calculator can give an answer, but not without the proper input. So come on. Give it input."

"Fine, I'll bite," Stonewerth said. "How are we going to bring down the force field?"

"We're not. It's about to go down by itself," Marco said. Everyone seemed surprised by this answer, Marco included. Why the hell would he have just said that? And yet somehow, in his mind he was convinced it was the truth. What was it he'd seen that led him to that conclusion?

Turning back to the holo-projector, he slowly flipped backward through all the videos and files he'd been looking at. He stopped at a recent clip of the prisms as they got closer to hatching. Staring at the image for a moment, he simply let his mouth move, giving voice to any random thing in his head.

"Proximity. The first prism opened quickly. Apparently it needed moisture. For whatever reason, that must be the best way to power the process. Then *we* were close. It tried to drive us mad. Again, I don't know how the science would work, but there it is. That was the second most efficient way to do the job. We know there has to be a third way, or else they wouldn't still be opening." Finally he consciously saw what his brain and mouth were unconsciously trying to tell him. "Look at some of these prisms, the ones that were only recently ejected from the gateway. They landed the farthest away, making them close to the generator poles, but despite being the last through, they're closer to hatching than many of the ones that came before. They're having an easier time feeding on some power source, and the poles are the only thing it could be."

"So those super long-lasting batteries in the poles…" Spam began. Marco nodded before he could finish.

"They're going to get drained, just like Weirdlust's body was drained. And once they're drained…"

"We can attack," Stonewerth said. "That's great, but we're still not going to have the advantage. First, there's already more hatched than we can easily deal with. Second, more will hatch before we can get through. And third, as long as there are still any prisms un-hatched out there at all, we're still at risk for going insane again. And the gateway will probably have spit out even more by that time. We'll be pretty helpless."

Marco let his mouth ramble on by itself again. "We'll gain back some advantage, but not enough. You're right. But there's something else here. I know it. Keep asking questions."

"Why do hot dogs come in packages of ten while hot dog buns come in packages of eight?" Tulip asked. Thorn gave her sister an incredulous look.

"Tulip, seriously?"

"Hey, weird questions might get us answers we wouldn't have gotten any other way," Tulip said with a shrug. Marco, despite his better judgment, let the question play around in his mind.

"I'd assume those are the numbers that are convenient for the manufacturers. It works for them, so they don't care if the numbers aren't compatible."

Thorn turned to Tulip. "See? That didn't do anything. So please stop…"

"Compatibility," Marco said.

Thorn looked back at him. "Huh?"

"Compatibility, compatibility. Something about compatibility," Marco mumbled to himself. Out of the corner of his eye he caught Thorn looking like she was about to ask another question, but Spam gestured for her to stop and let Marco keep going. "The alien technology we've seen is very advanced compared to us. It can derive power from moisture, from negative mental thoughts, from what we consider normal electrical power. It could draw power from other things, but all of it still needs a power source. Power source. Power source…"

He watched the live feed as the gateway discharged yet again. This time it sent enough prisms out that some went out of the direct range of the camera, so he couldn't be sure on the exact number. That would definitely be enough now to drain the generator poles. It would also be enough that they'd get easily overwhelmed by the army of alien convicts. But his peculiar brain forced him to go back to the moment of the discharge itself. When had the first discharge started? Soon after the gateway had put itself back together. What had powered the gateway putting itself back together? Their bits and pieces of madness were surely part of it, but that couldn't be it all alone. Something else had to have occurred at that time, some event using a different type of technology or power that they hadn't taken into effect before.

"Oh God," Marco said. "I think I get it. Stonewerth, when you started the hyper-space beam to communicate with command, it kept reaching a certain point and then starting over."

"Yeah," Stonewerth said. "So?"

"Did you ever turn off the comm equipment?"

"Yeah, of course I..." Stonewerth stopped as she thought back. "Maybe I didn't. I stopped trying to uplink with a hyper-beam, but in all the confusion, I think I left the actual equipment on." Understanding began to dawn on her face. "It's been on this whole time."

Marco nodded. "Starting right when the gateway had first been put back together. Do you all see? That's it. That's our answer. That's how we'll stop this. This whole time, we've been doing something to power it and send the alien prisoners through to us. What we need to do now is figure out how to reverse it."

17

"There's no outward sign of it," Doc said as she looked at the current feed on the holo-projector, "but according to the calculations I've been working on, we just passed the point where the prisms should have completely drained the batteries in the generator poles. We can be sure by watching the rate of hatching over the next couple minutes. If it's slower, then I'm correct."

Stonewerth was no longer directly at the door. The general consensus was that if the aliens suddenly decided to storm the Complex, the team would know. And if they made it into the building, it wouldn't matter if someone was guarding the door. Zeta Team might have had superior weapons, but the aliens had enough numbers to overwhelm them quickly.

"Do you think Fearless Leader knows yet that they aren't protected?" Stonewerth asked.

"It doesn't look like it," Marco said, pointing at the image. "But then, FL hasn't given us a lot to work with as far as reading its emotions or thoughts. Maybe he or she knows, or maybe not."

Thorn snorted. "Or maybe he's thinking up recipes for cheesecake."

"I'd be okay with that," Doc said. "It's been way too long since I've had cheesecake."

"If we all survive, I promise to buy cheesecake for everyone," Stonewerth said. "But can we focus for now? Let's go over the plan again."

"Okay, I'm going to be the one to undo the locks on the front door of the Complex," Spam said.

"And then once we're out, we waste no time getting over to the Hall," Thorn said. "No dawdling at all, in case that weird mind-screw power can work on us that fast and at that distance."

"Then once everyone is in the Hall, we barricade all the doors with some of the old bed frames," Tulip said.

"You, Doc, and I head into the comm room," Marco said to Stonewerth. "Doc finishes setting up the older comm array, and then sends out a signal telling Command what has been happening here. While she's doing this, you and I turn off the other comm equipment for the hyper-beam."

"And then?" Stonewerth asked.

Everyone shrugged. That was about as far as they'd been able to figure out so far.

"Good. Glad to know we're all on the same page," Stonewerth said with a sigh. As much as they believed their plan would work up to that point, that was where their knowledge of the situation failed them. Because turning off the hyper-beam signal completely might keep the gateway from staying powered up, but all of the aliens would still be outside. And at that point they would have realized that the force field was no longer there to protect them, so there wasn't necessarily anything to keep them from swarming the Hall. Stopping the gateway was all well and good, but unless they figured out how to make the gateway work in reverse, hopefully with the help of the hyper-beam equipment, they were still pretty much screwed.

"We shouldn't attack the aliens when we go out," Marco said.

"The hell we aren't," Thorn said.

"No, he's right," Spam said. "If we fire at them and they see the bullets go through where the force field used to be, then there won't be any incentive for them to stay in place. And as much as possible, we want them to stay grouped up. It will make them easier to pick off once we're sure the gateway is down."

"Right. Good thinking," Stonewerth said. "When we run across to the Hall, keep your weapons ready, but don't fire except at anything that crosses the force field line."

"Do you really think they've still got enough sanity to figure that out?" Tulip asked.

"Fearless Leader does," Marco said. "And that's all that will matter."

"Okay then," Stonewerth said. "Are we ready for this? Because if everything goes according to plan, this will be the easy part."

"Stone, we're Zeta Team," Spam said. "If the things we did went according to plan, none of us would be here."

"Way to rain on my parade, Spam," Stonewerth said. "Next time, leave the negativity to Thorn."

Thorn raised an eyebrow. "Somehow I am both proud and insulted at the same time."

"Move out, soldiers," Stonewerth said.

"Does that mean you want me to stay here now instead of helping?" Doc asked. "I'm not a soldier. Make up your mind."

"You know what I meant, smartass."

"No, I really didn't."

They all followed Spam out to the main Complex door. Once they were there, it took Spam several anxious minutes to undo the protections he'd set up at the door. Then, after all of them paused to take a deep breath, Stonewerth threw open the door and they all started running across to the Hall.

Their plan, as simple as it was, went wrong from the very beginning.

Later on, when Marco had time to contemplate what had happened, he remembered the prisms that he'd seen the gateway eject beyond the range of the camera. Could it be that Fearless Leader had seen the cameras and figured out exactly where their blind spots were? That seemed the most logical answer to Marco. The ones out of camera range would have likely been closer to generator poles, too, meaning they would have hatched faster. No additional aliens had come in from off screen to join Fearless Leader's growing group, which meant that they had to have gone somewhere else.

That somewhere else, it turned out, was around the Complex and the Hall, setting the team up for an ambush from a direction no one had expected.

Almost immediately once they were all out the door, two black shapes came hurtling at them from the direction opposite the gateway. Marco caught them out of the corner of his eye and spun, instantly firing. The others caught his movement and followed suit, but the aliens must have been prepared for this and darted out of the way. As they turned to face this threat, Marco heard something else coming from the direction of the gateway. He turned to see that two more of the creatures had gone out from their perceived shelter and were heading right for them, creating a pincer attack with the IPA soldiers in the middle.

"Move!" Stonewerth yelled from somewhere behind Marco.

"We're not going to be able to hold them off effectively if they're coming at us from both directions!"

Doing their best to keep up the suppressing fire at their back, Marco, Spam, Thorn, and Tulip ran in a back-peddling fashion over the rough surface of the planetoid. The four aliens bobbed and weaved, occasionally feinting in the team's direction to see if they could catch them off guard. Something about the pattern of attack felt wrong to Marco. If Fearless Leader was really watching and controlling all of this, the few brief moments where the team had been caught off guard should have been enough to send the rest of the aliens hurtling towards them, overwhelming the soldiers with their sheer numbers. Did Fearless Leader not think of that? Perhaps the creature was capable of thinking too highly of himself, believing he didn't even need to do such a thing in order to take out this meager resistance.

Or, Marco realized, there was still more to the sneak attack.

Marco whirled around just in time to see three additional aliens speed around the side of the Hall and come right for them. He aimed and fired, clipping one of them to send it sprawling, while the other two scattered.

It was now seven against six in favor of the aliens, with one wounded alien and one civilian human that didn't have any weapons. Marco would have liked to think that, for trained IPA soldiers, those were still good odds. In other circumstances, that might have even been the case. Here, though, it seemed like doom waiting to happen. He would be better off if he just sat down in the dust and waited for the end to…

Marco shook his head to try clearing away the thoughts. Out here in the open, the madness was trying to take over again. They had to get to the shelter of the Hall quickly. It wasn't that far. They could still all make it.

One of the aliens darted at them kamikaze style. Everyone fired, and many of the bullets hit, but the alien threw itself directly at them, apparently not caring that there was no way for it to survive this. The alien, already leaking blood and dying, hit Tulip square in the chest. She went flying, and two more of the aliens took that as their cue to go right for her.

"Oh no you don't!" Thorn screamed. She broke off from the

rest of the group and ran for Tulip, shredding one of the attacking aliens with a storm of bullets while the other dashed out of the way. Marco was torn for a moment between going to their aid and heading for the Hall. He couldn't just leave them.

As though she were expecting these thoughts from her teammates, Thorn gave a quick yell over her shoulder. "Everyone else, keep going! I can hold them off!"

Stonewerth barked the same command, which Marco instinctively followed. It was important that they reach the Hall. If they didn't, there was no other chance that any of them could get off the planetoid.

At the door of the Hall, Marco turned back to look, certain that he would see both Tulip and Thorn right behind them. He was horrified, then, to see that in the meantime one of the aliens had managed to get in a lucky swipe at Thorn's leg. She'd toppled next to her sister, who was still dazed and struggling to get up. Once she saw the state of her sister, though, Tulip crouched back down with Thorn at her back.

"Tulip, go! You can still make it!"

"But you can't," Tulip said. "I'm not leaving you."

"We don't even like each other!"

"Don't be an idiot. You're my twin sister. I love you, even if you are a downer."

The aliens swarmed around the pair, darting in loose circles around them and creating an impassable barrier between the sisters and safety. Marco checked to make sure his rifle still had ammo, then prepared to run for them.

Stonewerth grabbed him by the shoulder and yanked him back through the Hall's door. "No! What are you doing?" Marco asked. "We can still save them!"

Stonewerth just pointed beyond them to the gateway. Another five aliens had come out of the circle, moving swiftly for them. Marco's breath caught as he realized that Stonewerth was right. None of them would be fast enough to save Tulip and Thorn, and taking any more time to barricade the door would only result in putting the rest of them in greater danger.

Marco backed through the door, allowing Stonewerth to close it behind him as Spam pulled a bed frame over to act as a barricade. His last view of the two was of them sitting back to back, their rifles rattling as they released one last barrage. The colorful patches on Tulip's uniform stayed visible until they splashed full of blood red.

18

Even once they were in and the front door was shut tight, they still had several tense moments where they could have all died. The four remaining members of the team ran to each of the other outer doors to the Hall, checking to make sure that each one was secured against intruders. Most were fine, but the back door leading to the aiming range burst open right as Spam went to check the handle. One of the aliens attempted to slither inside, but Marco fired over Spam's shoulder and took the creature out. Working together, Marco and Spam shoved the alien's carcass back out of the way. They slammed the door and locked it just as something else banged into it. The alien on the other side tried this several times before it seemed to realize it wasn't getting through.

"This is bad," Spam said. "We don't have enough people now to keep a watch on all the doors."

"All the more reason to make sure those barricades are completely secure, or at least as secure as old bed frames can get," Stonewerth said. "Glare and Spam, you two go around and keep reinforcing every possible way they could get in here. Doc and I will do our best with the comm equipment."

Neither Marco nor Spam spoke to each other as they went around and checked. Marco was haunted by the image of the twins in their last stand, the aliens converging on them both just as the door shut. A part of Marco thought that maybe, just maybe, they'd been able to hold off the onslaught, but no. There had been too many, and in that last second as the door had slammed shut, Marco had seen too much blood. And it certainly hadn't been the pale blue blood of the aliens.

"There was nothing you could do," Spam finally quietly said to him.

"How exactly do you do that?" Marco asked him. "That thing where you always seem to know what I'm thinking?"

"Just a gift, I guess," Spam said.

Once they were certain the doors were all secured, or at least as secured as could be given the flimsy materials at their disposal,

Marco and Spam found themselves back in the main room. It had never been busy, of course, but now the place felt completely deserted. Shrug wasn't going to uncoil his lanky form anymore from his normal spot curled up on the couch. Neither Tulip or Thorn would bicker anymore over whether or not it was against the Sportsball rules to dump tacks down the front of their opponents pants. The majority of the beds still set up would no longer be the sight of regulation-violating fraternization. Over half of Zeta Team as Marco knew it was gone. He hadn't known them for long, but they'd all been stuck together in a situation that forced people to come to terms with each other quickly. So yes, they had all been his friends, even the ones he hadn't particularly liked such as Weirdlust. His only friends, really.

And before the day was done, there would probably be even more bodies.

Marco refused to let the sorrow hit him. Not this time. If he lived, there would be time for that later. Now was the time for looking at every angle of the situation and finding a way to keep themselves from falling to the alien invaders.

Stonewerth came out of the comm room first. For a moment, when she thought no one was watching, Stonewerth had a look of utmost weariness, like she too had seen too much death today and couldn't take anymore. But as soon as she realized she was being watched, Stonewerth adopted the hard, blank look of the senior officer tasked with keeping her few remaining soldiers alive.

"Is it shut down?" Spam asked her.

"It is. I even pulled a few key circuit boards to make sure it wasn't broadcasting anything we're not expecting."

Marco cocked his head. "What about your hand unit?" he asked. "Have you disabled that?"

Stonewerth sighed. "Shit. No. I'll go get it and take it apart."

"No, don't," Marco said. "I've got a thought. Bring it to me and let me look at it."

Stonewerth didn't question him. She just got the portable hyper-beam unit and handed it to him. As Marco fiddled with it, Doc came out of the comm room as well.

"The message is sent," Doc said. "They won't receive it for a while, but they will receive it. They'll know what happened here, but I don't know if they'll be able to help us. By the time we get a message back, this will all probably be over one way or the other."

"So what's the plan, then?" Spam asked. "There shouldn't be any more prisms coming through the gateway, and the force field is down even if Fearless Leader doesn't realize it. If we're going to make any kind of last stand, now would be the time, while we still have an element of surprise."

"Maybe," Stonewerth said. "Or maybe not. Given what you and Marco said about that alien you found in the Complex, they're probably really hungry after being imprisoned. Maybe if we can wait them out long enough in here, they'll starve. We have the food to do it."

"We'd be better off going back to the Complex," Doc said. "We would have more materials to work with there."

"I'm not sure that the four of us could survive another run across the way," Spam said. "Marco? What do you think?"

Marco barely heard him, but the question registered enough that it redirected his thoughts. His brain was working, doing its thing, processing, picking up various pieces. It was coming up with something, something crazy, something that would likely be his end, but he couldn't rid himself of the idea. He'd been a screw-up for his whole military career. He'd been useless, unwanted by everyone except Colonel Horitz.

But if the idea developing in his head was right, he could fix all that. He would be the one who could save everyone that remained.

It would mean he would die, of course, but that was his duty as a soldier in the Interplanetary Army. He was willing to give up his life if it meant that his last living friends stayed that way.

"Marco," Stonewerth said. "What's going on in that weird brain of yours?"

"Nothing, major," he said absently.

Stonewerth stared at him long and hard. Finally she looked away and said, "Okay then, for now we're going to do what little we can to get some rest. One person awake and doing a circuit of all the doors while everyone else tries to sleep, in one hour shifts. Glare, I'm giving you the first watch. Everyone else, grab a bed. Keep your weapons ready, though. They could send an attack at us at any time."

Marco thought everyone nodded, but he was still off in his own little world. His plan was formulating, and his position as first watch would allow him to execute it without anyone else trying to stop him. All he needed to do was wait for his moment.

He started to do his circuit of the doors, going around to the various points throughout the Hall and pretending that he was going to systematically check each one. Marco did one circuit, then stopped in the main room to check if he could hear or see any of the other three still moving. Doc was plopped face down in her bed while Stonewerth gave a soft, wheezing snore. Spam was the only one who didn't look like he was sleeping, as he fidgeted in bed. Hoping that this would be enough that none of them would notice what he was up to, Marco kept acting like he was checking the doors until he was once again in the mess hall. Here, moving as quietly as he possibly could, he broke down the hasty bed frame barricade and went out the door.

In the worst case scenario, one of the aliens would have been waiting for him just outside the door. Thankfully, from here, everything looked quiet. He could go around the Hall and approach the gateway, and if he moved with enough stealth he might be able to take a long way around and approach from the direction opposite of where Fearless Leader and the others were facing. He didn't think much of his chances of reaching the gateway from behind without any detection at all, but hopefully he wouldn't need to get that close.

If he was wrong, though, he would be killed out here all alone, and no one would know what it was he had intended to do. Suddenly he wondered at the wisdom of this plan. If he failed, the last best chance for the rest of the team would be lost, as he'd been too stuck in his ideas of saving them that he hadn't bothered to tell anyone what he thought he knew. He looked down at the portable hyper-beam unit in his hand, contemplating going back, when he felt the muzzle of a rifle press into his back.

Slowly, Marco turned around to see Stonewerth, Spam, and Doc all standing behind him. All of them, even Doc, had rifles at the ready. Stonewerth was the one with her weapon on Marco, although she hardly looked like she was going to use it.

"Sergeant Glare," she said quietly. "Do you mind telling us what you think you're doing?"

"I thought you were asleep," Marco said.

"I was faking it," Stonewerth said. "Not even you can notice everything all the time, especially when your mind is elsewhere. I knew you were planning something, so I waited, then got the others up. So I repeat my question. What the hell are you doing?"

"I think I have a way to end this," Marco said.

"And the reason you chose to sneak off and try this way by yourself rather than telling the rest of us?" Spam asked.

"Because… because I think the only way this could get pulled off is if the person doing it dies," Marco said.

Marco waited for some kind of shocked reaction from the others, but instead they all just nodded solemnly. "And you thought you were going to do this by yourself?" Stonewerth asked.

"Too many other people have died today," Marco said. "I knew that if I told you, you would all insist on coming with. And then you could die, too."

"Well? Are you going to tell us what this grand plan of yours is?" Spam asked.

"It's the hyper-beam unit," Doc said. "He thinks he has a way to use it against the gateway."

"The signal of the larger hyper-beam unit was causing the gateway to spit out the prisms," Marco said. "After fiddling with the unit a little bit, I think I can get it to work in reverse. It will pull all the prisms back in, right along with all the aliens around the gateway."

"That's great," Stonewerth said, although there was no cheer in her voice. "So explain to me why you couldn't do that with the larger unit back in the Hall? And why are you sneaking around if you can just reverse the whole thing?"

"I think I know," Doc said. "I might not have picked up on it as fast as Glare, but now that he's talking about it, I think it has to do with proximity."

"That's what I suspect, too. Everything we've seen so far suggests that proximity is important when powering the alien technology," Marco said. "The hyper-beam signal wasn't close enough to the gateway to make it work fast. We should be able to set up the signal so that now the gateway will work in reverse, but the main unit is too far away. It would be slow, about the same speed with which it's been spitting the prisms out. If we want to do it fast, all in one swoop, we need the signal to be closer to the gateway. The main unit is too heavy for that."

"I'm failing to see how this absolutely has to result in the death of whoever's doing this," Spam said.

"I do," Stonewerth said. "If someone is close enough to the gateway to make it work with any speed, then they'll also be close enough to get sucked in with all the aliens."

Marco nodded. "If that person can even survive the onslaught of aliens first."

"So you're going to sacrifice yourself?" Spam said. "You can't do that!"

"Someone has to," Marco said. "It's the only way to possibly save everyone else."

"But what about waiting them out?" Spam asked. "That should work."

"Spam, you know as well as the rest of us that such an idea was just grasping at straws," Marco said. "We'd be overwhelmed long before help could arrive. Reinforcements would arrive to find Zeta Team completely slaughtered down to the last person and a whole mess of aliens they would still need to mop up. And given how much damage the aliens have done so far, we wouldn't even be able to guarantee that all of the soldiers who show up to fight would get out alive, either. We all have to face the fact that the choice is one of us dying, or all of us plus more."

"But why you?" Spam asked. "I could do it."

"I couldn't ask that of anyone," Marco said.

"I'm certainly not volunteering," Doc muttered.

"Glare's right, Spam," Stonewerth said. "Normally I would say we draw straws, but it's his plan. He volunteered first. But I'll be damned if he's going out there to die alone."

"Stonewerth, no," Marco started to say. "The whole point is to minimize the number of people who have to die. If the rest of you come with me…"

"You'll have a greater chance of actually reaching your goal," Stonewerth said. "If you go alone and you fail, that means others are going to have to try replicating what you wanted to do. This way, not only will you have the rest of us covering you, but if you fall then one of us can take the hyper-beam unit and finish what you started. You know I'm right, Glare. I can see it in your eyes. And also, I'm still your God-damned commanding officer, and if we're going to go with your crazy suicide plan, then we do it according to my rules. Is that clear, Sergeant?"

"Crystal, Major."

"Fine then. Show the rest of us what you need to do with the hand unit, just in case."

Marco went over how to reverse the signal on the unit with them all. There was a heaviness in his heart, knowing that the rest of his friends might now die along with him, but also an intense love for all of them. However this ended, they were all going to do it together as a team.

19

Huddled behind the Hall, each of them aware that an alien could come around at any moment and blow their cover, they did their preparations for the final assault. Marco found it ironic as Stonewerth passed out a large number of magazines for their rifles while the aiming range was in plain sight nearby. Apparently all that ammo hoarding had been worth it after all, as they were going to need as much as possible now.

Once they all had fully loaded weapons and knew the basic plan of attack, they started off in a wide arc that would eventually arch back and come up behind the gateway. Although it added a lot of time to their journey, taking the long route would allow them to come up from an unexpected direction and use the natural curvature of the small planetoid to hide their approach. They would come up over the horizon behind the gateway far, far closer than they ever could on a real planet like Earth. From there they would simply try to be quiet and unnoticed by the aliens for as long as possible. Once the aliens became aware that the humans were coming from the exact opposite direction of where they were expected, Zeta Team would do one final direct run at the gateway. While Marco did indeed have a rifle of his own, it would be the job of the other three to take out anything coming for him as he ran directly for the gateway. Once he was close enough, or when it looked like he might be eviscerated by one of the aliens, Marco would activate the portable unit. The others would hopefully be far enough back that they wouldn't get sucked in, and Marco would hopefully get close enough that the gateway did its thing quickly. That was way too many "hopefullies" for anyone's liking, but that was the nature of last ditch attempts. They would succeed, or else they would take out as many of the aliens as possible in the process of their own deaths.

As they quietly made their way around to their last stand, Marco noticed as Stonewerth and Spam seemed to fall behind. Although they were trying to do it as surreptitiously as possible, it became obvious soon after to Marco exactly what was going on.

When the two of them separated again, Marco made it a point to go over to Stonewerth and have his own conversation with her.

"I know what you two were just talking about," Marco said in a voice that neither of the others would be able to hear. Stonewerth didn't look happy about this, but neither did she look surprised.

"I figured you might," Stonewerth answered, although she didn't say anything more, leaving Marco to say the obvious.

"You were talking him out of trying to take the hyper-beam unit and take my place," Marco said.

Stonewerth paused for a long moment before responding. "How did you figure that out? That funky brain of yours doing its thing again?"

"Didn't need to," Marco said. "As much as he hates the title, the rest of the human-inhabited galaxy still calls him the Robin Hood of the Outer Colonial Worlds. He's exactly the kind to try something like that. He thinks he needs to save the universe, like somehow it's his job."

Stonewerth raised an eyebrow at him. "And isn't that what you're intending to do?"

"It's not about whether I need to be the hero. It's simply that someone has to do it. I'm the one who came up with the plan, so I'm the one with the moral obligation to do it. I don't have the right to expect anyone else to do it."

They stopped walking. They could see the top of the gateway just over the rise. They could continue trying to sneak the rest of the way from here, but all it would take was a single alien facing the wrong way. They decided it would be better if they started their charge from here, running the whole way. Or at least most of the way. Marco explained what he thought might be a safe distance once the gateway was reversed, and made sure that none of them would cross that line: a spot roughly twice the distance from the gateway to the surrounding line of generator poles.

"You can't get any closer than that," Marco said. "If we're lucky, that will also be enough distance that you won't have to worry about the madness taking over, either. You're going to have to stay back and simply provide cover fire. Once I cross that line, I will have the hand unit ready. If it looks like I'm about to go down, I'll activate it, but the closer I get, the more likely this is to work. Everyone got it?"

"We understand completely," Spam said.

"One hundred percent," Doc said.

Stonewerth stepped forward and offered Marco her hand. It was an oddly formal gesture, considering how intimate they'd already been otherwise, but Marco gladly accepted it. "It's been an honor working with you, Sergeant. Your name will one day be spoken with reverence in the history of the Interplanetary Army. Of that I have absolutely no doubt."

Marco nodded. "Okay then. Let's do this."

They all turned in the direction of the gateway. Marco clipped the hand unit to his uniform, making sure the button to activate it was ready for him to hit at a moment's notice. Then they all readied their weapons, took deep breaths, and started their final charge.

They hadn't had a chance to get a look at the current state of the aliens and prisms before they had snuck out the back of the Hall, but it appeared that the gateway had made one last discharge of prisms before they'd shut down the main hyper-beam unit. None of them had hatched, at least, nor did they look like they were getting close to that point. Most of the previous prisms, however, had already disgorged their occupants, who were now milling around the gateway. None of them gave any indication that they knew the force field was down, nor probably would they until something tried to get in and didn't bounce off in a flash of static. Also, they were all facing the direction of the Hall and the Complex. Zeta Team did, in fact, have several moments of surprise. It was the rare occasion where something worked in their favor instead of against them.

Not that the situation stayed in their favor for long. Only a few seconds after Marco saw the aliens, one of them seemed to sense their presence and turned around. For a moment it didn't seem to know what to do about the team of crazed humans charging directly at them. It raised a silent alarm among the others, though, and all the aliens, the shorter form of Fearless Leader included, turned in their direction.

The aliens didn't look particularly worried. It wasn't until Stonewerth started firing, with the others close behind on her signal, and the bullets crossed the invisible barrier with no problem, that any of the aliens seemed to realize they were in trouble.

The automatic fire of the rifles wasn't terribly accurate from this distance, but the aliens were initially grouped so close together that accuracy wasn't important. Blue blood flew in all directions before the aliens scattered. Marco noted with some satisfaction that Fearless Leader took a particularly large number of bullets and fell over. Although the alien still moved, that could only work to Zeta Team's advantage if the closest thing the intruders had to a mastermind was injured and down. Indeed, there didn't seem to be any pattern or reason to the way the aliens got out of the way of the attacking force.

Or at least that was the way it was at first. After the initial moments of confusion, the aliens took their turn to attack. While a number of them stayed back, several dashed forward directly at Marco. He took out one easily, while the other members of the team wounded several more. Those aliens went around behind, trying to create a pincer, but Doc, while hardly the best shot, managed to herd them into Stonewerth's line of fire.

Over the gunfire, Marco heard Spam say something. "Hey, um, everyone? I'm starting to get hungry."

"This really isn't the time for that, Spam," Stonewerth said. "Too many snarky, inane comments and I'll have you drop and give me twenty."

"No, that's exactly what I mean," Spam said. "I'm getting *hungry*."

Marco understood his meaning completely, as the rifle in his hands started to feel like a weight holding him down. He just wanted to drop it, to fall to his knees, to let darkness completely overcome his thoughts. He fought back against it, though, even as he noticed that one or two of the closer prisms were pulsing.

"We're in range for the madness to start affecting us," Marco said. He fired at an alien that made a feint toward him. At the last second the alien dodged to the side, backing off before trying to come around from a different angle. Spam shot it, blowing one of its arms off in a spray of blue, and the alien backed off for the moment. "This is where you guys have to stop. You can't afford to get any closer."

"We've still got about eight meters before the safe distance, though!" Doc said. "Don't make me get out my tape measure and check!"

"We need to get closer if we're going to effectively cover you," Stonewerth said.

"No!" Marco said. "This is where you have to stop. This is where…"

"Spam, do it!" Stonewerth yelled.

The aliens had pulled back, although they could rush forward again at any moment. It would be irresponsible to do anything but press their advantage. That was why Marco was shocked as Spam dropped his rifle and instead grabbed Marco from behind by both arms.

"What… what the hell are you doing?" Marco asked. Doc kept firing wildly, rarely hitting anything but keeping the aliens from getting too close, as Stonewerth came up to Marco and calmly unclipped the hand unit from his uniform.

"I'm the commanding officer here, so I'm doing whatever needs to be done," Stonewerth said.

"No, Stonewerth, you can't!" Marco said.

"Why not? I meant what I said, Glare. You're destined to be remembered. You have it in you to do great things. The IPA needs you, whether they know it or not. But me? I've had my time."

Major Stonewerth clipped the hand unit to her own uniform, then turned with a savage scream and ran for the gateway.

Spam let go so he could pick up his weapon again. Marco followed Stonewerth for several steps, but she moved too fast for Marco to catch up with her and take the hand unit back. With an apparently easy target heading right for them, the aliens that had been going after their group instead concentrated on Stonewerth. Marco cursed, then did the only thing he could. He provided cover fire as his superior officer ran to her death.

The next minute was a blur of bullets and screaming and alien blood. Stonewerth ran and dodged, stopping only to shoot any aliens that made it past the attacks of the others and got closer to her. Several times the aliens got close enough to swipe at her. Sometimes red spatter would flash through the air at this, but each time Marco, Spam, and Doc concentrated their fire and took out the attacker. Stonewerth crossed the boundary that Marco had originally determined then had to slow down in her approach as she went deeper in the swarming tide of aliens. Marco realized now that he probably wouldn't have even made it, given the nature of what the gateway did to him. He probably would have toppled over and curled up into a ball long before he got anywhere near the gateway. Stonewerth didn't have the same problem. Instead she cursed and screamed at every approaching alien, telling them to drop and give her twenty or threatening to have them court-martialed for insubordination. At one point her cybernetic leg gave out on her right next to a prism, likely the result of the prism draining its energy in an attempt to hatch.

Then she was there. Stonewerth was right in front of the gateway, alien bodies falling around her even as more prisms hatched. She unclipped the hand unit, held it in the direction of the gateway, and went to press the button.

Before she could, four sets of claws ripped across her back. Stonewerth toppled to her knees in surprise, the hand unit falling from her hand and bouncing about a meter away. Behind her, Fearless Leader stood in a pose that almost looked triumphant, his pale blue blood smeared now and mixed with Stonewerth's red.

Marco didn't hesitate. Knowing that lugging his rifle with him would only slow him down, he dropped his weapon and sprinted as fast as he could directly for Stonewerth and Fearless Leader. Spam and Doc both screamed from behind for him to stop, but Marco ignored them. All his attention stayed focused on those two combatants ahead of him and the device on the ground.

Aliens rushed him. A hail of bullets flew from behind him, taking them down.

Depression overcame him. Hatred and self-loathing tried to break his mind, but he fought it.

Prisms hatched around him. He ran past, narrowly dodging as a few new alien attackers went at him.

Everything around him tried to stop him. Marco avoided it all. He was the adoptive son of Colonel Horitz. He was an IPA soldier. But most importantly, he was a part of Zeta Team, and Zeta Team didn't let the piddly little fact that they were all screw-ups bring them down. All his fallen teammates today had proven that, and Marco was going to honor their memory.

Fearless Leader, although terribly wounded, still had enough energy to leap over Stonewerth's prone form and come straight for Marco. Marco's brain slowed everything down. He picked up every clue and detail in his environment. And there was one detail that apparently Fearless Leader had missed. Instead of continuing to run right at the alien in a crazy game of chicken, Marco stopped, letting Fearless Leader close the distance.

Marco, however, didn't watch Fearless Leader come for him. Instead he looked beyond at Stonewerth. Despite what Fearless Leader might have assumed, Stonewerth wasn't dead. She was still breathing, and Marco knew that as long as she breathed, she would still fight.

Stonewerth, summoning one last burst of strength, pushed herself back to her feet just long enough to launch herself at the hand unit. Marco turned, forcing his weary body to run back with the same determination with which he'd come at Fearless Leader.

At this exact moment, Marco knew he was within the danger zone. He had maybe seconds at most to get back out of range of the gateway, but he couldn't go too fast. He wanted to be safe, but Fearless Leader needed to stay within the zone.

Behind him, something flashed bright, brighter than any of the times previously when the gateway had discharged its prisoners. Spam and Doc were both forced to drop their weapons and shield their eyes.

From behind him, Marco felt the pull of the gateway. He heard ungodly noises from the aliens, then a strange sucking sound that repeated over and over. Marco assumed this was the sound of the aliens and prisms, maybe even the generator poles, being pulled back through the gateway with whatever mysterious alien physics powered it. Even closer, Marco heard the hiss of Fearless Leader first getting nearer, then being pulled back along with everyone else. Marco couldn't dare look back, though. If he did, he would lose precious momentum. Despite pushing himself as hard as he could, Marco felt himself slowing, his feet slipping every time they hit the ground and tried to propel himself forward. He was close to safety, but not close enough.

Someone grabbed his right wrist with both hands. Marco looked up to see Spam in front of him, desperately trying to keep his footing as he pulled at Marco. Doc came up right behind him, grabbing Spam by the waist to further anchor him.

"What, you didn't seriously think you were going to get to be the hero all by yourself, did you?" Spam asked. Through all his straining, he smiled. Marco smiled back.

It was a smile that disappeared almost immediately when he looked down at Doc and Spam's feet. They were sliding in the gray dust of Planetoid Shithead. For all their effort, the three of them were still being slowly pulled into the gateway.

Marco grunted. His legs gave out beneath him and he fell. Although Spam didn't let go, it was enough to make all of them lose their precious traction.

Doc fell over, knocking down Spam right along with her. With nothing else to hold them in place, all three of them hurtled back in the direction of the gateway.

Marco closed his eyes.

There was a sound like a roar, or maybe an explosion. Marco fell to the ground and lost consciousness.

He couldn't have been out for long. When his senses came back to him, Marco sputtered through a face full of dust. He wasn't moving. Nothing was yanking him from behind. Both Spam and Doc lay on the ground with them, the two of them just as equally disoriented as Marco.

Marco forced himself to his feet and then turned to look at the gateway.

It was gone.

In its place were the ruins. They were exactly as Marco remembered seeing them when he had first arrived on 54174340, right down to the patterns they made and the slight glowing of mysterious alien letters.

"What happened?" Spam asked as he sat up.

"The hand unit was powering the gateway," Marco said. "It would have gotten sucked in with everything else. Without it, there wouldn't be anything to keep giving the reversed gateway any power."

"But why did the ruins revert back to the way they were?"

Doc asked.

"I don't know," Marco said. But then, maybe he did. With all its prisoners back, or at least the ones that weren't currently corpses beyond the range of the gateway, the prison had gone back into lockdown mode.

The aliens and Fearless Leader were gone.

And so was Stonewerth.

20

Every inhabitant of Planetoid 54174340 stood waiting at the landing site as the troop shuttle *Milwaukee* touched down on the surface. Once the ramp was down, a steady flow of IPA soldiers poured out. They were all battle-ready, although Marco had sent a message much earlier that all the fighting was over. It had been over for nearly two weeks now. But the IPA apparently wasn't taking any chances. For all they knew, the message Marco had sent using the outdated comm equipment was some kind of decoy from the invading alien race. Marco wasn't surprised then that their back-up forces touched on the planetoid ready for combat. What did surprise him was the man who walked down the ramp once all the soldiers were out.

Marco stood at attention and saluted as Colonel Horitz stepped foot in the planetoid's gray dust. Spam, having gone longer without needing to follow protocol, hesitated before he did the same. Doc joined them, even though she was a civilian and had no such obligation.

Horitz saluted back. "At ease, soldiers." Horitz looked tired, like he'd somehow been awake for the entire journey instead of spending it in hyper-stasis. It took Marco a second to realize that the colonel had been worried. He'd sent the closest thing he had to a son to a place where he should have been so safe it was boring. Instead Marco had been part of the first ever battle with an alien species that had wiped out the majority of the Zeta Team.

Screw protocol for once, Marco thought. He grabbed Horitz and hugged him tightly. There was murmuring from a number of the troops waiting nearby.

For several breaths nothing happened. Then Horitz hugged him back. When they stepped away from each other again, Horitz looked much more relaxed. Marco might even go so far as to say that he looked proud.

"Private Cruz, I'm here to give you your full debrief," Horitz said. "Command thought I might be the most appropriate person for the job."

"Sergeant," Spam muttered.

Horitz looked at him with a raised eyebrow. "What was that, soldier?"

"Sir, you're addressing Sergeant Cruz. Major Stonewerth gave him a battlefield promotion before she…" Spam trailed off, probably unsure what to say. Horitz nodded sympathetically.

"Yes, of course. I knew Major Stonewerth. She was an excellent soldier, even if she did spit on me once."

Marco blinked. "You… you're the one who…"

"She mistakenly believed that I had acted on some bad information that got her and several other soldiers hurt. It was above her pay grade to know that the person actually responsible had already been taken care of. I couldn't tell her, but I could send her somewhere where I thought she wouldn't have to worry about combat anymore. Sadly, it appears I was mistaken."

"She served well, colonel," Marco said.

"I have no doubt that she did. If you don't mind, the troops are going to spread out and make sure the area is secure. Not that we believe it isn't, but you understand that we have to be sure. Once they've done that, they'll start to settle in at their new outpost, and the expanded science team will disembark when they're given the all-clear. While that's going on, I do believe you three have quite the story to tell."

They did indeed. While they had spent much of the time waiting for reinforcements with recording everything that had happened, they still tried to leave no detail out as they gave Colonel Horitz a rundown of everything that had happened. The tale took long enough that they decided to wander around between the two buildings as they spoke. Horitz listened to everything, interrupting only twice, once to clarify a small detail and once when they led him into the Hall. All the beds had been put back in their proper place in preparation for the new troops, but the colonel still noticed something out of place with the floor.

"What exactly is this white strip of paint here?" he asked.

"I believe that's the foul line, sir," Marco said.

"No, that's the goal line," Spam said.

Doc shook her head. "You're both wrong. That's the free-throw line."

"There's no free-throw line in Sportsball," Spam said.

"No, I think she's right," Marco said. "There is a free-throw line, but only on alternate Thursdays and holidays that begin with a Q."

After that, they brought Horitz into the Complex and showed him the room that had originally been Weirdlust's lab. They'd converted it into an approximation of a morgue in which to store the alien bodies. Following the battle there had been two still left alive that hadn't been sucked back through the gateway, but they had been injured. One had died of its wounds soon after, while the other, while Marco and the others had been trying to figure out how to detain it for when the next wave of scientists came to study it, had tried to attack them and gotten killed for its trouble. The room was starting to smell pretty rank, as they didn't have the proper equipment to keep the bodies cool to prevent rotting, but they'd done their best. New equipment for that, as well as much more, would be arriving within the next few days. 54174340 was not going to be a forgotten outpost full of obsolete equipment anymore. Starting soon, the top secret installation would be the more important research station in the human-occupied portions of the galaxy.

A smaller room, much easier to cool, had been converted temporarily as a morgue for humans, but it was empty now. Those bodies had been moved. Once the remaining members of Zeta Team had finished with their story, they took Horitz to the cemetery.

After some debate among the three of them, they had decided to bury their comrades at the point where they had started their final attack. Not only did it have that special meaning, but it was also out of the way enough that bodies wouldn't have to be moved once more buildings were put in to support the large number of troops and researchers who would now be making this place their home. There was still a lot of debate as to where the best place for such things would be, as close proximity to the ruins could still have adverse mental effects on some people, but that wasn't for Marco, Spam, and Doc to worry about. They had purely been concerned with allowing their fallen teammates their proper rest.

They had spent much of their time waiting for reinforcements with crafting the four small tombstones and one larger memorial block that marked the cemetery. With Weirdlust's body completely disintegrated and Stonewerth vanished, they had only needed to dig graves for Hamlet, Shrug, Tulip, and Thorn. There had again been some debate as to what names would go on the tombstones before they had decided that the individual stones would have just their nicknames while the main memorial would have more. Colonel Horitz stopped in front of the memorial and read it in silence.

In memory of those members of the Zeta Team who were lost during the Battle of Planetoid Shithead:
Chelsea "Stone" Stonewerth
Thorn "Tulip" Murphy
Tulip "Thorn" Murphy
Robert "Shrug" Odwall
Marcus "Hamlet" Spencer
Victor "Weirdlust" Graven
Somehow, it was still less dangerous than Sportsball

Horitz looked like he was struggling somewhere between a smile and a frown. "I'm not sure how comfortable I am with you using this as a way to officially name the planetoid as Shithead."

"Anything less would be to dishonor their memory," Doc said.

Despite the solemn moment, Marco had to fight desperately not to laugh.

"Thank you very much for showing me this," Horitz said to Spam and Doc. "But now I think it's time that I had a chat with Sergeant Cruz alone."

"Actually, could I trouble you for something first, colonel?" Doc asked.

"What is it?"

"You see, if you would just be willing to wait here while I get my tape measure, I would very much like to measure your…"

"Doc, that's really not a good idea," Spam said.

The two of them left, giving Horitz and Marco a moment by themselves.

"Do I want to know what she was about to ask?" Horitz asked.

"No sir, you really don't."

"No one else is around, Marco. Call me Jake."

Marco smiled. "Yes sir."

Horitz smiled back. "You did it. You really did it. I knew you would find your niche eventually."

"I did, sir, although at great cost."

"Of course. And all your fallen comrades will be properly honored, even if the cause of their death is going to have to remain a secret for the time being. The name Zeta Team will now be given the respect it deserves."

"I think they would have liked that," Marco said, gesturing to the tombstones.

"Now for the thing I really wanted to discuss with you, Marco. What are you going to do next?"

Marco cocked his head in confusion. "Sir?"

"I suppose you haven't been told yet. Command was impressed with you. So impressed that they went back over your record and took a closer look at some of the incidents. As it turns out, in a few of them you averted some disasters."

Marco was too surprised to respond.

"That brain of yours must have picked up on things that no one else could see. The chicken incident? After further study, our scientists found a previously unknown virus incubating in their systems. You prevented a plague, Marco. And as for the hat thing, well, that's still classified, but I think you at least deserve to know that you prevented a complex chain of events that would have resulted in a nuclear explosion."

"You have got to be kidding me?"

"I can't make this shit up, Marco. It's all true. Everything else in your record is also being reanalyzed, and along with your performance here, it's been decided that you're being wasted. You're to be promoted, far higher up than just Sergeant, and I have it on good authority that you will be given your pick of assignments."

Marco took a long moment to compose his thoughts. "Sir, that is an honor, and I am grateful to you and everyone who believes in me."

"I sense a 'but' there, sergeant."

"But if I get my pick of assignments, I would really like to stay here."

"Here?" Horitz asked incredulously. "Here on the ball of rock you people have dubbed Shithead?"

Marco gestured for the colonel to follow him. As Marco talked, he led Horitz in the direction of the ruins.

"This is where I think I'm most needed, sir. I'm the one who originally cracked the code on the ruins, and I think there is more I can do. We need to study the alien bodies we have. We need to see what we can find out about their culture. We need to figure out how their technology works. This is my home now. This is where my gift can flourish the most."

Horitz smiled. "I can see the logic there. I'm sure I can convince others that you're absolutely right. What about the other two? They're going to be getting a similar offer."

"I can't speak for them for sure, sir, but I'd be surprised if they wanted to leave. There's still a member of Zeta Team that needs rescuing, and we would all like to work on that together."

Horitz frowned. "What do you mean?"

"Let me show you, sir."

Marco led him to the stones in the ruins. They still pulsed with symbols, and on occasion they would still let off an electrical discharge, but the cycle wasn't as frequent now. Marco found a specific stone and had Horitz look at the symbols that appeared there.

"We noticed it three days after the final battle," Marco said. "Take a look."

The alien symbols pulsed, but they weren't alone now. In addition to the many alien handwritings and dialects, there were now also letters clearly recognizable to humans.

"We've decided that each of the alien symbols must represent letters that identify specific alien inmates locked beyond the gateway. We still don't have any idea how they work, but that's what the new batch of scientists are for. With their help, Spam, Doc, and I hope that we can find a way to get her out."

"Her?" Horitz asked. "What do you mean? What are these letters supposed to represent?"

"Sir, when you rearrange them and put them in the right order, they spell 'Drop and give me twenty.'"

Horitz smiled again. "Yes. I see what you mean. Well then,

Sergeant, it looks like, from now on, you're going to be in charge around here. How about you go meet the newest members of Zeta Team?"

Marco said that he would like that very much.

THE END

SEVEREDPRESS

 facebook.com/severedpress
 twitter.com/severedpress

CHECK OUT OTHER GREAT SCIENCE FICTION BOOKS

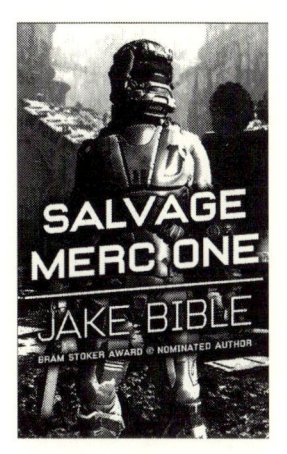

SALVAGE MERC ONE
by Jake Bible

Joseph Laribeau was born to be a Marine in the Galactic Fleet. He was born to fight the alien enemies known as the Skrang Alliance and travel the galaxy doing his duty as a Marine Sergeant. But when the War ended and Joe found himself medically discharged, the best job ever was over and he never thought he'd find his way again.

Then a beautiful alien walked into his life and offered him a chance at something even greater than the Fleet, a chance to serve with the Salvage Merc Corp.

Now known as Salvage Merc One Eighty-Four, Joe Laribeau is given the ultimate assignment by the SMC bosses. To his surprise it is neither a military nor a corporate salvage. Rather, Joe has to risk his life for one of his own. He has to find and bring back the legend that started the Corp.

SERENGETI
by J.B. Rockwell

It was supposed to be an easy job: find the Dark Star Revolution Starships, destroy them, and go home. But a booby-trapped vessel decimates the Meridian Alliance fleet, leaving Serengeti—a Valkyrie class warship with a sentient AI brain—on her own; wrecked and abandoned in an empty expanse of space. On the edge of total failure, Serengeti thinks only of her crew. She herds the survivors into a lifeboat, intending to sling them into space. But the escape pod sticks in her belly, locking the cryogenically frozen crew inside.

Then a scavenger ship arrives to pick Serengeti's bones clean. Her engines dead, her guns long silenced, Serengeti and her last two robots must find a way to fight the scavengers off and save the crew trapped inside her.

SEVEREDPRESS

facebook.com/severedpress
twitter.com/severedpress

CHECK OUT OTHER GREAT SCIENCE FICTION BOOKS

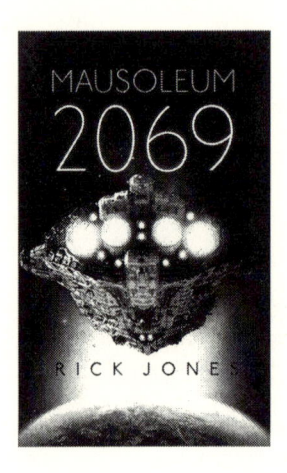

MAUSOLEUM 2069
by **Rick Jones**

Political dignitaries including the President of the Federation gather for a ceremony onboard Mausoleum 2069. But when a cloud of interstellar dust passes through the galaxy and eclipses Earth, the tenants within the walls of Mausoleum 2069 are reborn and the undead begin to rise. As the struggle between life and death onboard the mausoleum develops, Eriq Wyman, a one-time member of a Special ops team called the Force Elite, is given the task to lead the President to the safety of Earth. But is Earth like Mausoleum 2069? A landscape of the living dead? Has the war of the Apocalypse finally begun? With so many questions there is only one certainty: in space there is nowhere to run and nowhere to hide.

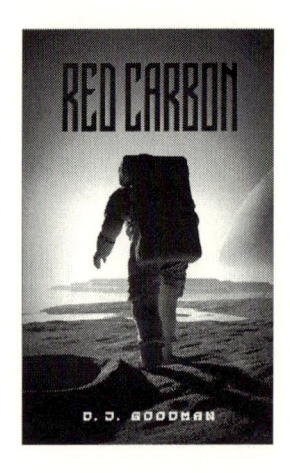

RED CARBON
by **D.J. Goodman**

Diamonds have been discovered on Mars.

After years of neglect to space programs around the world, a ruthless corporation has made it to the Red Planet first, establishing their own mining operation with its own rules and laws, its own class system, and little oversight from Earth. Conditions are harsh, but its people have learned how to make the Martian colony home.

But something has gone catastrophically wrong on Earth. As the colony leaders try to cover it up, hacker Leah Hartnup is getting suspicious. Her boundless curiosity will lead her to a horrifying truth: they are cut off, possibly forever. There are no more supplies coming. There will be no more support. There is no more mission to accomplish. All that's left is one goal: survival.

SEVEREDPRESS

facebook.com/severedpress
twitter.com/severedpress

CHECK OUT OTHER GREAT SCIENCE FICTION BOOKS

IN PERPETUITY
by Jake Bible

For two thousand years, Earth and her many colonies across the galaxy have fought against the Estelian menace. Having faced overwhelming losses, the CSC has instituted the largest military draft ever, conscripting millions into the battle against the aliens. Major Bartram North has been tasked with the unenviable task of coordinating the military education of hundreds of thousands of recruits and turning them into troops ready to fight and die for the cause.

As Major North struggles to maintain a training pace that the CSC insists upon, he realizes something isn't right on the Perpetuity. But before he can investigate, the station dissolves into madness brought on by the physical booster known as pharma. Unfortunately for Major North, that is not the only nightmare he faces- an armada of Estelian warships is on the edge of the solar system and headed right for Earth!

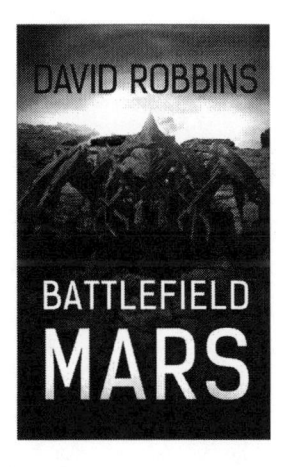

BATTLEFIELD MARS
by David Robbins

Several centuries into the future, Earth has established three colonies on Mars. No indigenous life has been discovered, and humankind looks forward to making the Red Planet their own.

Then 'something' emerges out of a long-extinct volcano and doesn't like what the humans are doing.

Captain Archard Rahn, United Nations Interplanetary Corps, tries to stem the rising tide of slaughter. But the Martians are more than they seem, and it isn't long before Mars erupts in all-out war.

Made in United States
Orlando, FL
18 December 2021